# The Giraffe is Free

## by Nick Delmedico

*An Eighth Day Village of the Sun Saga*

**Published by**

**Copyright ©2022 by Nick Delmedico**

Contact: halfabook@dplus2.com

All characters in this book are fictional; any resemblance to persons living or dead is purely coincidental. The Eighth Day Village of the Sun and New Maya City of Worlds are also fictional, created by my good friend Randall Rex Harrison, a man who believes that intentional communities are the next step in human growth and development. At the time of publication these places do not exist, except perhaps in our hearts. Moholo.

Manufactured in the United States of America

The Giraffe is Free

Fiction

Action and Adventure

ISBN 978-1-58884-018-9  (print version)

     978-1-58884-019-6  (eBook version)

# Introduction

I have always been an idealist. I believe in a better future, the nobility of mankind, and the right of everyone to live their lives in the manner they choose, as long as it does no harm. I'm no Miss America, but I think that world peace is a good thing. My Christian upbringing tells me that the meek will one day inherit the earth, that swords will be beat into plow shears, and that mankind will find a new purpose in life, something more in line with our spiritual destiny.

As a young man I fell in love with James Hilton's vision in *Lost Horizon*. Shangri La was more than a hopeful dream. For me, it was an ideal worth believing. The hawks and warmongers tell me that the technology of battle trickles down to the common man, that war is necessary. Are there really any benefits? I think about all the achievements that have been destroyed by war, the buildings, the art, the books, and the great ideas. During the siege of Syracuse, Archimedes, one of the greatest thinkers of his time, was killed by an errant soldier despite being told to spare his life. When will we realize the cost of war goes beyond lives and money?

When Randall Rex Harrison came to me with the idea for *Free the Giraffes* I was already living in an intentional community. It was easy for me to buy into his vision. I have seen what like minded people can achieve when they work together. The Eighth Day Village of the Sun was a natural outgrowth of my dreams. I had already seen such a place in my imagination. It was easy to put it down on paper. Building such a place was another thing. Randall had done more than me. He had a prospectus, a budget, and a vision for a population that needed physicists, animal specialists, builders and house cleaners, right beside priests, pranic healers, and bartenders. He had gone as far as creating a budget of $630 million dollars (1998 figures) to build such a community.

All ideas begin with a vision. I helped him give life to his ideas in the first book but the vision did not end there. The dream called to me again. This time it was not content to thrive in the obscurity of my imagination. It needed a place in the real world. If nothing else, I have tried to make it real. To that end, this story is dedicated to all the idealists, all the dreamers, all who hope for a better world. May we all find our Shangri La.

Nick Delmedico, September 2022

# Chapter 1

## Step Into my Parlor

"How soon before we get there?" asked Tinker. "We've been driving through this forest for some time."

"Rothschild likes his privacy," said Simian. He kept his mind on the road, piloting the car over the twisting, winding route. "This used to be a National Park until he bought it and converted it to his private estate."

"Oh," said Tinker. "So, how did you meet him? How did you meet the richest man in the world?"

"He sought me out," said Simian proudly, a broad smile spreading across his face. "He needed my skills."

"My skills, you mean," said Tinker.

"Our skills," said Simian. "We're a team."

They drove in silence, Tinker staring out the window at the passing scenery. Soon they arrived at a guard shack with a gate. Several phone calls were made by a Uniformed Man as they were swarmed by minions clamoring over the car and their belongings. They were checked and rechecked, searched and researched, their pockets emptied, a thorough look through the car, all under the scrutiny of the Uniformed Man.

"We found this, sir," said one of the men as he reported to the Uniform.

"That's my computer," said Tinker.

"We'll need time to check it out thoroughly," said the Uniform. "Mister Rothschild insists. Don't worry. It will be returned to you later."

Tinker started to protest but Simian pinched him. "It's okay," he said to the Uniform. "Check it out. There's nothing sinister in there," he chuckled.

The Uniform did not join him in brevity. Instead he stepped back and waved his hand. Minions swarmed again, this time opening a gate with obvious ceremony. "Follow the main road until you come to a house," he said. "Mr. Rothschild's butler Gort will see you in." The Uniform turned his back on them and stepped away. A minion motioned for them to drive on and they did.

"That was intense," said Tinker.

"I hear he has a security department the size of a small army," said Simian. "Rothschild doesn't like uninvited guests or surprises."

"Why did you let them take my computer?" asked Tinker.

"You heard him, they need to check it out. Besides, I don't think we had a choice."

"But it has all my private data on it, including the software for our demonstration."

"Relax," said Simian. "You'll get it back. If not, you can whine to Rothschild about it. Please just act like an adult and stop complaining. I got us this gig. We both stand to make a lot of money off this."

Tinker stared out the window again wondering what he had gotten into. When had Simian become so greedy? Sure, money was great to have, but at what cost? He had no idea what Rothschild wanted, but something told him it would not be pleasant.

The road twisted and turned as they climbed in elevation. Finally they rounded a bend where the landscape opened to a tree lined lake. Ahead was a mansion that put any to shame, three stories high with ornate decor and woodwork. Huge windows protected by bars stood twelve feet high attesting to the size of the first floor. Balconies stood out prominently on the upper floors. On one Tinker thought he saw a stout man staring out across the lake.

The double door to the main entrance opened like the gates to an ancient city. Out stepped a tall man, the butler Gort, dressed perfectly for the part. He motioned for Simian to pull into a nearby parking space then turned and walked back into the mansion leaving the doors open.

Simian opened the trunk.

"They took all our luggage too," said Tinker.

"What luggage? A backpack and a ditty bag. Don't worry about that now," he said, pointing towards the open front door. "We need to follow the butler."

Gort stood quietly in the vestibule. He saw them coming and he turned and walked down a long corridor that ended in an elevator. They quickly followed. Once summoned, they took the elevator up to the third floor. Again they walked down a long corridor, this one lined with faceless doors. Gort stopped in front of one and stared at Simian as he opened it. "You might want to freshen up before your meeting with Mr. Rothschild," he said.

"Hey, how did my luggage beat me here?" he asked, spying the familiar ditty at the foot of the bed. Gort didn't answer, just led Tinker to the next room. "Mr. Rothschild will see you in an hour. I will call for you then."

Tinker shut the door behind him, glad to be rid of the creepy butler. He ran to the bed and began inspecting his backpack. It was obvious it had been searched, the contents probably dumped out, groped, and then stuffed back with no respect for the owner. He laid down on the bed, again wondering what he had gotten into.

Simian was his friend, but there was a  limit to what friends can do. He had been pressured to come along with him on this gig as a technical expert. Simian specifically wanted Tinker to bring along his computer containing proprietary government software.

His thoughts drifted until he heard a knock at the door. "Mr. Rothschild is ready to see you now."

Tinker composed himself, wondering if he should have changed his shirt. He really didn't know what the butler meant by 'freshen up', nonetheless he followed Gort down the lengthy hallway to the creepy elevator. Once they landed on the first floor, he followed him through a maze of hallways and rooms. Finally they arrived at a double door that Gort opened with a flourish. Tinker entered, the door closing with a loud click behind him. He glanced backwards noting the butler was just inside and to the right, standing at what seemed to be a relaxed attention.

Ahead of him was a table, broad and polished. On it there were two silver platters with silver covers over the contents. Across the table sat a fat man, enormous by weight, partially reclined in a large padded chair. Facing the man and seated with his back to him was his friend Simian.

"Please join us," said the fat man, his arm extending toward an empty seat. On the table in front of it was Tinker's computer.

Simian stood up and clapped his friend on the shoulder. "Tinker Thompson, I have the pleasure of introducing you to our benefactor, Mr. T. Harmon Rothschild."

Tinker leaned forward, a gesture of respect more than anything. He could hardly reach halfway across the broad table to shake hands, and Mr. Rothschild did not make any effort to do so either, so he took his assigned seat.

"Your friend and I have been talking about the marvelous work you are doing for our Government," said Rothschild.

"It's top secret work, Mr. Rothschild," said Tinker.

"So I hear," said Rothschild. "You work at that installation near Tonopah, am I right?"

"Yes, sir."

"I know all about your secret project," said Rothschild. "You are not the only one that works there."

"My friend Simian works there, too," said Tinker.

"As do many others," said Rothschild. "Now, if we can get down to business. You're here to give me a little demonstration of the system you have been developing."

"I don't know if I can do that, Mr. Rothschild," said Tinker. "As you said, it's top secret."

"Of course it is," said Rothschild. "I have the proper clearance and I own several of the companies that developed and put the satellite systems in place. You are here to demonstrate that the software you have been developing links up to my satellites properly and performs the task it was designed to do."

"We've already tested that," said Tinker. "Everything appears to working properly."

"Good," said Rothschild. "Then you'll have no problem with this little demonstration."

Tinker hesitated.

"It's okay," said Simian. "Everything checks out." He slid the computer closer to Tinker.

"Why aren't we doing this demonstration in a secured government facility?" asked Tinker.

"This is a secured facility," said Rothschild. "Or didn't you notice?"

There was a grunt of agreement from Gort.

"Okay, okay," said Tinker. He hunched over the computer and turned it on, his fingers dancing over the keyboard. Windows opened and closed, passwords and gates were passed and secured. Simian watched everything with careful eyes. Rothschild leaned back and relaxed. The chair hummed as it massaged his body.

"What exactly do you want me to do?" asked Tinker.

"As I said, a little demonstration," said Rothschild. "Start with an explanation of the system and its purpose."

Simian stood up. "Well, as you know, Mr. Rothschild, weather can be unpredictable."

"Sit down and shut up," said Rothschild. "I want to hear it from Mr. Thompson."

Tinker nervously cleared his throat. "I can give you the long explanation about satellite controls, ground sensors, thermal focus, isobaric thresholds, but what it comes down to is a system for weather control. No more melting ice caps. Rain on demand, where it is needed. We are even experimenting with controlling forest fires by changing wind dynamics. There are limitless possibilities."

"Does one of those possibilities include creating tornadoes, hurricanes, and floods?"

"The military has already expressed an interest in that aspect of our project," said Tinker. "They always look for a way to weaponize scientific research."

"I see," said Rothschild. "All I want is a little demonstration that it works."

"I can assure you, it does," said Tinker proudly.

"Then show me," said Rothschild.

"What would like to see?" said Tinker. "Snow in the Sonoran desert? Tropical sunshine in Seattle?"

"All too common," said Rothschild. "I have something extraordinary in mind."

"Name it," said Tinker.

Rothschild slid a piece of paper across the table. "These are coordinates."

Tinker took them and entered it into the computer. "This seems to be a remote location on the coast of Mexico."

"Yes, it is," said Rothschild. "I want you to create a small hurricane, force five on the Saffir-Simpson scale, and direct it to that location."

Tinker looked up from his computer. "I don't know if I can do that. A force five hurricane? It could harm millions of people."

"Which is why I want the storm to affect only this location," said Rothschild. "Only this location."

"Not sure I can do that."

Simian turned to his friend. "Do you mean it is not technically possible, Tinker, because I know it is." He turned to Rothschild. "We've made storms over remote areas. Big ones."

"Why don't we just change the location for the test?" asked Tinker. "We could check the shipping lanes and make a short lived storm at sea."

"That's been done. I have already seen that demonstration," said Rothschild. "It's why I wanted you here. To test it further." He smiled benignly. "I'm quite interested in the effect over land."

Tinker took a deep breath. "I just don't feel right about it, Mr. Rothschild. Storms over the Sahara, polar ice caps, even the uninhabited parts of the Pacific, I'll do those in a minute. I can't knowingly threaten human lives."

Rothschild frowned and turned to Simian "It seems your friend is unable to continue. Can you complete this task, Mister Jacks?"

"For what you're paying us, of course I can." he pushed Tinker aside but his friend refused to let go of the computer. They struggled over it until Gort appeared from behind and twisted Tinker's arm. He let go of it and Simian pulled it away. "I don't know what's gotten into you, Tinker."

"This is not what we agreed."

"You agreed to come here and get paid," said Simian.

"You said it was a consulting job, maybe some demonstration software."

"That's exactly what it is," said Simian.

"Please, please, gentlemen," said Rothschild. "In good faith, let me show you I am a man of my word." He leaned forward from his chair and pushed the serving trays on the table toward them. "One for each of you."

Simian lifted the cover. There were neat stacks of bills, all taped and counted like fresh bank money. His eyes lit up. "A man of your word," he said, his speech soft and reverent as if he were in church.

Tinker stared at the money, thoughts churning in his head like old laundry in a front loading washer. *What if Rothschild wasn't lying about his security clearance? Surely my friend Simian checked all this out. He did insist that the work was legitimate. He needed my help, cut me in on this deal. So much money! I would be a fool to walk away from this when success is so close. But, ahhh, the agony! A force five hurricane! A whirlwind of unstoppable destruction. Coastal flooding. Windspeeds over a hundred and sixty miles per hour.*

Tinker's breath grew short. Simian clapped his friend on the back rubbing it gently for a moment. "You all right buddy?"

His breath calmed. He looked at Simian, then eyed Gort standing nearby.

Rothschild nodded and the butler took the computer from Simian and placed it in front of Tinker. The fat man leaned close. "I'll ask you again. What's it going to be, Mr. Thompson? Will I have my demonstration?"

# Chapter 2

## A Typical Eighth Day

Randall stood beside his trusted giraffe Anji. He pet her gently on the side. "Are you ready for a ride this morning?" he asked.

The giraffe gently lowered her head and nudged Randall. She was strong and he fought to keep his balance as he wrapped his arms around her neck. With a hug he said, "Yes, yes. I'm ready too. But first we must stretch. Open our muscles before activity. That is the secret of a healthy body. Let's stretch and release the stored toxins of the night."

He released her and did a yoga pose, launching into his favorite Kriya, a breath technique that energized him. Anji snorted, imitating him, almost as if she understood. He did ten minutes of yoga, a routine he had practiced daily for years. Later there would be more, but in his opinion this was the only way to start his day.

That and a ride on the beach with Anji. He mounted his giraffe and guided her out of the paddock.

As he looked towards the surf he could see dolphin leaping, flipping in the air to land on their backs. Schools of ballyhoo broke through the water into the air, flying fish that hugged the surface until they disappeared under the waves.

He looked the other way, dense jungle left untouched, a natural zone necessary to the survival of the village. Anji slowed as they passed a waterfall dropping from a cliff into a tidal basin. A crane waded through the water looking for fish to eat. Thirsty animals stood nearby, ocelots and javelina, tapir and monkeys. Randall passed a jaguar feeding her young. He saw birds and squirrels shake the treetops with their movements.

Villagers respected the animals and allowed them their space, just as nature allowed them space to build their village. The animals were never hunted. When they wandered into civilization they were met with psychics, backed up with animal control specialists. They are treated much like a lost tourist. The safety of the animal is just as important as the safety of the humans.

Anji picked up speed again. Randall felt the wind in his face, heard the surf at his side, smelled the jungle odors that hung on the breeze. The sand scattered under heavy hoof beats. Living in the moment, this was heaven to him.

They slowed down as they came to an open hut, Manny's beach bar, a popular spot in the Eighth Day Village of the Sun, especially with tourists. Manny only had one customer, but as soon as he heard the sound of hooves he went to work preparing a mango smoothie. When it was done he clamped it to a tray on a long pole which he raised toward the mounted rider.

"Good morning Randall. How are you today?"

Randall took the glass from the pole and drank deep. "Excellent, Manny," he said.

"Something for you too," he said to Anji. He lowered the pole and pushed a barrel of leaves towards her. "I know you can out eat anyone in the city, so have at it."

She didn't wait for the invitation, her head dove into the barrel.

"Where are you off to today?" asked Manny.

"South, my friend. The sun is up and I'm anxious to ride." He took another deep drink of the smoothie watching Anji dig into the leaves. "Fresh leaves?"

"I keep my hut clean," he said. "And why waste these as compost? I planted an acacia tree just for her."

Randall took another drink and tossed the empty glass to Manny. "What about your guest?" asked Randall, indicating the lone customer at the bar. "I've seen her here all week. I know you're always looking. Could she be the future Mrs. Manny DuBois?"

"A worthy candidate," said Manny. "If I don't get back to her she may lose interest. I, on the other hand, have not lost interest. There is so much more to her than I have uncovered."

"A week wasn't enough?"

"It would take a lifetime with this one," he said.

Anji raised her head from the empty barrel. "Time to go, then," said Randall. "Hyaa! On Anji!"

The giraffe took off, Randall gripping the reigns as she cantered away.

Manny turned his attention back to the beautiful blond sitting at his bar. She had on a bathing suit, a beach wrap, and embellished sandals that made her painted toenails pop with color. He moved to a stool beside her. No need to be on the other side of the bar. She picked up her smoothie and moved it to her mouth. He followed every movement, right up to where she puckered her lips and put the straw between them. Her beach wrap was open and his eyes moved from her lips and down the length of her body.

Behind him he heard someone clear their throat and say, "Before you go any deeper, Manny, could you do me a favor?"

Manny swung around for a look. Without hesitating, he punched him in the arm.

"Ouch! That hurt."

"Sorry," said Manny. "I had to see if it was really you." He turned towards the blond. "Caroline, this is Cameron Singh."

"Pleased to meet you," she said politely. She turned towards Manny with a scowl. "Why did you hit him?"

"He's always popping in and out. I didn't hear him coming so I suspected he was astral projecting."

"What do you mean?" she asked.

"I have the ability to focus my attention wherever I choose," said Cameron. "So focused that I can project the form of my body as if it were solid."

"It's not real, it's an ethereal body," said Manny. "You can't really touch it."

"It is real," said Singh. "If you were a reincarnated Atlantean like me, aware of your past lives, then you would know that I am my own reality, just as real as you."

"If you had been projecting then my hand would have gone right through you," said Manny. "I've done it before."

"Why do you not accept my astral form?" asked Singh. "You're the only one in the village who has to check."

"Your astral form does not order drinks," said Manny. "Now that you're here, can I make you a smoothie?"

"I need more than that," he said. "A vitamin supplement smoothie for starters. Some provisions for my outing today."

Manny hopped behind the bar. "Coming right up."

"What else can you do beside astral project?" asked Caroline.

"I remember all my past lives and incarnations. That's what brings me to my mission today. Last night in my dream form I replayed an episode from an incarnation I had as an Aztec priest. Oddly enough, though, the details have been slowly fading from my consciousness."

"What do you mean?" she asked.

"I can't remember what I dreamed or what I learned last night," he said. "I'm not used to this. I have an eidetic memory, capable of recalling things in great detail."

"You were an Aztec priest in a former lifetime?" she asked.

"I'm not sure," he said. "Maybe."

"Interesting," she said. "Are you also psychic?"

"Isn't everyone?" said Singh.

She laughed. "Certainly I'm not."

"Are you so sure?" he asked. "You seemed to be reading Manny's mind okay."

"You don't have to be psychic to read me," said Manny. He placed a bag on the bar in front of Singh along with a sealed cup of smoothie. "So, where are you off to today?"

"The dense jungle east of here," he said. "There is a temple out there, that much I know, with something in it that I need to recover. I'm hazy on the details."

"Most of the ancient pyramids and temples have been found and mapped," said Manny. "Lidar and GIS have made jungle expeditions obsolete."

"Not this one," said Singh. "This place has escaped detection. The temple has a huge presence in a higher dimension, easy to see when you have the Sight."

"Good luck then," said Manny. "Don't wear out your shoes."

"I reserved an air car," said Singh.

"Isn't it dangerous tromping through the jungle? Snakes and panthers, stinging bugs," said Caroline. "Why not astral project out there? Wouldn't it be safer?"

"Like I said, there is something there I need to recover. I won't be able to pick it up without being there in person." He picked up the cup and the bag as if demonstrating. "My soul has called me to action. I would be a fool to ignore it." He turned to Manny, "Thanks for the food and drink." He nodded to Caroline, slid off the stool and walked away.

"What an interesting character," said Caroline.

"Lots of characters around here," said Manny.

"And you're not one of them?" she teased. "I know all about your crystal experiments. Now you're an expert at Lidar and GIS?"

"I have my hobbies."

Again she puckered her lips and took a sip of her drink. "This is my last day here, you know" she said.

"You should do something special," he said.

"I agree," she said. She put the cup down on the bar. "Do you have something in mind?"

With the straw out of the way, Manny moved closer.

"You can come with us," said a voice beside him.

"Barclay McKenner," said Manny. "Your timing is..."

"Impeccable?" he added. "I think in ten more minutes I would have found the bar closed for the day."

Manny looked back to Caroline while talking to him. "You're probably right. Just as soon as I take care of the morning rush here at Manny's Beachside Bistro."

"Who's your friend?" asked McKenner.

"May I introduce Caroline Garmen."

"Of the Dechutes Garmens," said Caroline.

"We've already met, but not informally. You were with a tour group that passed through our meeting hall."

"I remember you Mr. McKenner," she said.

"Call me Barclay. Any friend of Manny's is a friend of mine."

"And where are you off to today?" asked Manny. "Another trip to the dolphins?"

"My research continues," said Barclay. "These creatures are intelligent. We have much to learn from them."

"I know," said Manny. He turned to Caroline. "Maybe you should go with him today. It would certainly be something special."

"Is that what you want?" she asked.

Manny took a deep breath. "No," he said. "I would rather you spend your last day with me. I've thought of calling Philippe and asking him to watch the bar today. He's done it many times."

Caroline turned to Barclay. "Then I'm afraid I have to disappoint you, Mister McKenner."

Franklin Van Dorn appeared beside him toting equipment and carboys. "It's okay, Barclay," he said. "I'll still go with you."

"Caroline Garmen," said Barclay. "My fellow researcher, Franklin Van Dorn."

"Pleased," she said, offering her hand. Van Dorn was gallant, instead of shaking it he took it and gently kissed it on the back. "I'm sorry you won't be joining us."

"I'm afraid I have a previous engagement," she said, turning towards Manny. The bartender's smile widened as he stared into her eyes.

Van Dorn put a carboy on the bar. "Can you fill this with papaya juice?" he asked.

Manny took a moment to break his glance with Caroline. He went behind the bar, Van Dorn quickly taking his place on the stool beside Caroline. Manny positioned the carboy under his juice dispenser and filled it. "Anything else you need?" he asked, placing it on the bar between Caroline and Franklin.

McKenner laughed. "How about a couple of sandwiches?"

Manny took a bag, went to the cooler and filled it with food. "Yesterday's leftovers," he said. "But I also put some fresh fruit and power bars in there." He passed the bag to McKenner then moved back around the counter. Standing beside Van Dorn he said, "I think you're in my seat."

Van Dorn looked at Caroline. "I think he's right," she said.

Van Dorn turned towards McKenner. "I guess then, we'll be off." He picked up the carboy and slid out of the seat. Manny was quick to replace him.

"Have fun, boys," said Caroline, turning her attention back to Manny.

"We will," said McKenner. "Come on Barclay. Don't you know it's rude to stare."

"I just hope I have better luck attracting dolphin today."

After they were gone Caroline eyed Manny much the way he did her. His Hawaiian shirt was open to the waist revealing his crop of dark chest hair. Beneath his shorts were tanned legs, tight and muscular, firm as tree trunks. His dark brown eyes held her interest even more, mysterious orbs that led to his soul. She could become lost in them for days, had been. All this, and he was utterly charming, more than a simple bartender.

"How about you make that call to Philippe," she said.

# Chapter 3

## The Choice

"The demonstration, please?" asked Rothschild.

Tinker stood up. "I don't want any part of this," he said. "You can keep your money but I'm taking my computer." He reached for it at the same time Simian did. A tug of war began. Gort appeared again, his meaty hands taking it from both of them.

"Give me back my computer," Tinker demanded.

Rothschild was calm. "So, you seem to have made your decision. Of course you are free to go, Mr. Thompson. Your computer will be waiting for you at the gate when you get there. See to it, Gort. And get his things for him." The butler left, carrying the computer with him.

"I can pack for myself," said Tinker.

"Nonsense," said Rothschild. "Let my butler do it for you. That's why I pay him."

Tinker went to the door but it was locked. He returned to the table and calmly took a seat.

"You're being a fool," said Simian.

"So are you," said Tinker. "I just hope you realize what you're doing."

Simian looked over at Rothschild, then at the tray of money. "I know what I'm doing. I'd hoped you would join me on this deal. There's still time." He looked over at Rothschild. The fat man nodded in agreement.

"Think about what you're doing," said Tinker. "A force five hurricane. Think about how many lives will be affected when it hits the mainland."

"It's okay. The target is a remote part of southern Mexico." he said. "Not the U.S."

"And when it goes inland?" he asked. "What if it hits Mexico City?"

Simian stared at the money. "If you feel that way you can donate your half of the money for them to rebuild."

Rothschild laughed.

"Will money bring back the dead?" asked Tinker. "I'd rather they not be impacted to begin with."

"What a humanitarian," said Rothschild. The doors opened and Gort entered carrying Tinker's backpack.

"Your belongings," said Rothschild. "And now, if you will excuse us."

Gort dropped the backpack on the table. He covered the money and removed the tray, placing it on a small table in the corner of the room.

Tinker sat there for a minute taking in the scene. He stood up, hoisted the backpack over his shoulders and turned to exit. "How am I going to get home?" asked Tinker. "I drove here with you."

"My guards will have a taxi waiting for you at the gate," said Rothschild. "Gort, give him five hundred dollars."

Gort lifted the lid on the tray that was formerly for Tinker. The money was neatly piled. Tinker stared at it, his mind in contemplation. Gort ripped a pack of bound cash open and peeled off five one hundred dollar bills.

"Cab fare," said Rothschild "Give him another five hundred, Gort."

Gort handed him the money.

"For your troubles, Mr. Thompson," said Rothschild.

Tinker turned to Simian. "I guess I'll see you back at the base, then."

"Keep quiet about this, buddy," he replied. "It never happened."

"Yes, yes," agreed Rothschild. "Top secret meeting, as you said

22

earlier. Mister Jacks and I will be staying. I'm afraid you'll have to walk to the guard shack. It's not far. Gort will show you out and point the way."

Tinker hesitated, then turned and left the room.

"Now," said Rothschild. "I hope you can finish this demonstration."

"I can't do it without the computer," said Simian.

"Yes," said Rothschild. "We'll take care of that. I'll have Gort bring you another computer when he finishes with Mr. Thompson. You told me weeks ago at our first meeting that you could do this."

"I can," said Simian.

"Then why did you bring your friend into this?"

"He is an artist, Mr. Rothschild. I am an amateur playing with blocks compared to him. He has the most experience with the software and can craft the perfect storm. All I can do is promise to do my best."

"That is all I expect," said Rothschild.

∂∞

Gort opened the door and practically shoved Tinker outside. Caught off balance, he stumbled down the steps. "Follow that path across the street," said Gort. "It leads down the mountain and to the guard shack." The door closed with a final thud.

Tinker looked around. He thought about checking his backpack, decided it was useless. They could have kept everything and he couldn't complain. He opened the top flap nonetheless, spotting his phone in the place he always kept it. That was all he needed, as anyone who has lost their phone can attest. It's the modern wand of power.

He put the phone in his top pocket, tightened the straps on his backpack and began to walk.

The path was narrow in places, following the lake until it turned and wound between forest and rock. He could hear birds chirping in the trees, wildlife rustling in the branches. He was not much of an outdoor man and the sounds only made him nervous.

"No one should go hiking by themselves," he said out loud. His voice was swallowed by the dense woods, muted to near silence. The sound of animals echoed back at him, louder than his own voice.

"Wonder how much farther it is," he said.

He stopped and took out his headphones from a side pocket in his backpack. Covering his ears with them he plugged them into his phone. The sound of the jungle was soon replaced with selected music.

Music to soothe the savage beast?

Not quite. He came to a clearing, his steps keeping pace to the beat of the music. He forgot another rule of hiking. Besides being prepared, having spare clothes, food, and other such things, there is a rule about being aware of your surroundings. With music blaring in his ears, he didn't hear the trees crack and shake behind him as he entered the meadow. As he followed the well worn path across the open space, he didn't hear the heavy breathing behind him. Had he checked his backpack, he would have found a piece of rotting meat bundled with his clothes. Oblivious to the environment, he felt only his own footsteps and not the thud of heavy claws shaking the ground, at least not until it was too late.

The bear stood high, roaring as Tinker turned around. One swipe with his claws opened a gash across the hiker's neck. Tinker screamed until the bear leaned forward across him, smothering him in fur as the beast tried to claw at the backpack. The bear roared furiously, turning the wounded man over in his massive paws, gnawing at the backpack until the full weight of the animal crushed his spine. The bear roared again, the trees in the meadow quaking and cracking as the wind carried his song of victory.

ॐ∞

Gort entered the room, placing the computer in front of Simian.

"I thought you were bringing this to the main gate for Tinker," said Simian.

"He's on foot. We have plenty of time," said Rothschild. "You can proceed with the demonstration."

"But I don't know his passwords, his codes," said Simian.

"Give him the printout," said Rothschild.

Gort produced a piece of paper and set it beside the computer.

"I installed a keystroke logger as a contingency. I am a strong judge of character, Mr. Jacks. Plus I did my homework. I had Tinker Thompson investigated as soon as you suggested using him. I suspected he could be compromised. I'm afraid I'm a better judge of character than you." The fat man leaned back in his chair. "Would you like a drink, Mr. Jacks?"

"I think I'll need one," said Simian.

Rothschild nodded to Gort who went to a nearby bar. He returned with two double whiskys poured over a minimal amount of ice. Simian took a gulp and went to work. Rothschild relished the moment. His command over men, his power wielded with something a simple as money. Make no mistake, he had plenty of power.

"I programmed the demonstration. Tinker already had the coordinates set. I think I'm ready to execute the command."

"Go ahead," said Rothschild.

Simian pushed the button. It was as simple as that. Like a bombardier, he had delivered his death message to a distant set of coordinates. What would happen next was up to satellites and sensors, wave generators and infrared converters. He watched a small window that displayed a radar image of the target area. Soon, clouds began to form offshore, signs of cyclonic action. He smiled, turning his attention to the money still laying on the table. "It's happening, sir," he said.

"Good," said Rothschild. "If you wish, you can count the money while we wait to see the results of your demonstration."

Simian moved the computer aside, pushing it to the center of the table. Both of them could see the screen now. A sidebar to the radar image showed estimated windspeed increasing. Cloud density was forming around an eye. Blocks of rain could be seen.

Rothschild smiled. "The sun is about to set for the Eighth Day Village."

"What was that?" asked Simian.

"Nothing," said Rothschild. "Just thinking out loud."

There was a knock at the door. Gort opened it. It was the Uniform from the front gate. "Sorry to disturb you, Mr. Rothschild. There's been a terrible accident."

Rothschild was nonchalant. "Oh?"

"Your guest," said the Uniform. "He never made it to the gate. We sent a party looking for him."

Simian turned to face him.

The Uniform looked at Simian, reporting the facts in an unemotional voice. "As improbable as it seems, sir, he was mauled by a bear."

"Mauled?" said Simian, rising to his feet.

"Yes, sir," said the Uniform. "We've notified the authorities."

"Is he okay?" asked Simian.

With the face of an angel and the sincerity of the devil the Uniform said, "He's dead. I'm afraid the bear made off with the backpack."

"Ah," said Rothschild. "Lucky we still have the computer. Thank you Louis."

The Uniform turned and left, Gort acting the perfect doorman, locking it behind.

Simian stood in shock. "My friend is dead?"

"I'm sorry," said Rothschild. "Truly I am. He was a good man, a principled man."

"Mauled by a bear," said Simian.

"Well, this was a national park at one time," said Rothschild. He took a drink of the whiskey, adding, "And Baba Randall is not the only one who surrounds himself with wild animals."

# Chapter 4

## Rough Seas

Franklin Van Dorn strapped on a mask along with the special lightweight rebreather that McKenner had invented. Once underwater it never ran out of air, extracting precious oxygen from the water like gills on a fish. Using microchips and sensors it expertly mixed the oxygen with his spent carbon dioxide to a suitable breathing mixture. Nitrogen in the air was extracted from the sea as well, pumped and processed by a band that surrounded his chest. As his lungs expanded and contracted so did the band, providing mechanical action necessary to operate the extractor. There were pressure sensors in the apparatus as well. As he dove deeper the mixtures changed to beneficial nitrox, allowing him more time underwater with a wider margin of safety.

The dolphin were out already, surrounding him and the boat, splashing in playful and friendly gestures. He held onto a trailing line while Barclay McKenner secured the boat and got ready to join him.

Barclay donned his own rebreather and let his mask hang free around his neck. "The skies are clouding up," he said. "Funny, the weather report called for clear skies."

Franklin rolled over on his back and stared upward. The clouds seemed to be moving fast, like you'd see in a speeded up filmclip from an old Hollywood movie. It was almost unnatural.

A sudden gust of wind hit him from the west. The boat lurched and Barclay grabbed onto the gunnels to steady himself. He scanned the skies again. "Now where did that come from?"

The clouds turned from billowy white to dark gray in an instant. A light rain began to fall building with each new rattle of lightning and thunder. Barclay shouted over the rain to Van Dorn. "You'd better get back aboard."

Franklin tugged on the line, gripping it as tight as he could. A strong current threatened to pull him away from the boat. The wind gusted again and the craft tilted. Barclay lost his grip and fell into the center of the open boat.

Franklin shouted, pulling on the line to make his way closer. The waves began to cap, tall ones that tried to pull the line out of his hands. It worked in cadence with the current, conspiring to yank him further away from the boat. He wished he had worn gloves, the rope burned and the salt water added to his distress. The wind began to howl, the sea churning and tossing with increasing fury. "Barclay!" he shouted. "Barclay! Help! Reel me in."

Inside the boat his friend lay helpless at the bottom. Water splashed over the sides, the deck becoming slippery and wet. He tried to get to his feet but was slammed against the side as the boat pitched and tossed him about like beans in a sack. The wind howled and the noise of the churning sea made it difficult to hear. "Hang on Franklin," he shouted. "I heard you the first time. I'm coming to pull you in."

He flipped around, crawling towards the back of the boat like a child. He reached for the line and slipped again, sliding towards the bow of the boat. Again he struggled, painfully making his way towards the stern. He reached for the line, managing to get a grip on it before the boat tilted again. The rope slid between his hands, slipping like the reel of a salt water pole with a fighting fish on the line. He opened his arms and hugged it, drawing it close to his chest so as not to lose it. When he finally got a grip on it again the line was slack. He pulled on it until he saw the end of the line come tumbling over the stern, empty.

He started yelling, his words swallowed by the dense rain and surging waves.

Franklin Van Dorn was at the mercy of the sea. The dolphin had long ago abandoned him. The boat was drifting away. He saw it as he rode the cresting waves to the top, catching glimpses of it getting further away as he struggled to swim towards it. But the sea had other ideas. It gave him one final view of the boat before it swept him away. It had capsized, turned upside down by the violent whim of an angry ocean. The heavy stern was trying to pull it down, the nose bobbing up and down. He couldn't tell if there was anyone on board.

The sea tugged at him again. Tired of shouting, his throat sore, he put the rebreather in his mouth and sank beneath the waves. Darkness engulfed him as he bobbed below the surface, trying to think about what to do. His thoughts were mainly of his friend, lost at sea. He finally decided there was nothing he could do about it.

He had his own problems now.

# Chapter 5

## Free the Giraffe

"Slow, Anji," said Randall. "Calm down girl."

The weather had grown unexpectedly rough. The tide came in quickly, trapping Randall and Anji on a sand bar. He tried to get her to cross a slough and move closer to the beach but she refused.

"You can lead a giraffe to water but you can't make them swim," he said, gently petting her neck, trying to calm her increasing anxiety.

The water rose to her ankles. She felt unsteady in the shifting sand under her feet. There was no choice but to cross the slough to safety, but like a stubborn mule the giraffe refused to budge.

Randall got down from his mount, the water reaching well above his knees. He gripped the reigns and stepped off the sandbar and into the slough.

Anji complained, rearing her head and bucking like a scared bronco. Randall calmed her, now up to his waist in water. "Come on, girl," he said. "See? It's safe."

There is something between an animal and its companion. Trust is a big part of it. Led by Randall, Anji nervously stepped off the sand bar and into the slough. The longshore current was swift and the tide continued to rise unexpectedly fast. Randall moved quickly, now up to his chest in water. The current formed holes of sand around his feet with every step. "Keep moving Anji, or else we're stuck."

Anji snorted following Randall who gripped her reigns tightly. They passed fish and crabs caught up and swept along by the current. Anji reared up at the sight of them but Randall held her steady. He felt the slope rising. "We're here, girl," he said. "Just a few more steps."

Soon they were on the beach and not a moment too soon. It was a narrow stretch of sand bordered by a steep rock wall that blocked them from going further inland. Randall studied the sea. White caps dusted the surface of the water and the waves began to swell. They began to steal the sand away moving closer to the cliff walls. He looked up and saw a cave. "We'll be cut off soon," he said to Anji. "I can sit it out in that cave but you'll have to make a run for it. Do you understand?"

She neighed, snorted, and bent down low. Randall took the reigns off her. "You're free," he said. "Run back to the village. Look for a safe place to hide until this is over. I'll find you."

She snorted again.

"I know. Now run! That way!" He swatted her gently with the reigns and she took off, her feet splashing in the surging waters. "Good luck," he said. He looked up toward the cave, studying the cliff face for a path up to it. There seemed to be a sloping ledge, narrow but not impassable.

Water sloshed at his feet, the waves claiming the last of the open sand beneath him. "A little longer and I'll be able to swim to the cave." A wave struck him broadside, "If I'm not dashed to pieces against these rocks."

He struggled, found a foothold, and hoisted himself up and onto the ledge. His feet slipped and he thought about removing his sandals, a difficult maneuver in his present position. He looked up and sideways towards the cave. He couldn't see the opening from where he was. He felt strong winds against his side threatening to rip him off the rock face. He did a quick Kriya, a breath technique that helped him focus. "Trust the universe," he said out loud, reaching out for another handhold.

Continuing blindly, groping his way across the ledge, rain began to fall heavier. Rivulets of mud started to trickle down the cliff face. His clothes were wet but now they became heavy with mud. He looked over his shoulder, twisting his head. It was a long way down to the ground, a drop that would surely injure him, breaking bones on the exposed rocks. He moved his feet again, inching along the ledge, breathing slowly to stay focused.

His arms ached. Reaching for the next purchase, he felt nothing. With one final effort he pushed himself sideways and fell into the opening of the cave.

Exhausted, he rolled onto his back on the soft, muddy floor and fell asleep.

ᚥ∞

Hours later he awoke choking, his face half submerged in water. The storm raged outside, rain was pouring through the open entrance of the cave making it look like the back side of a waterfall. The ledge acted as a funnel, directing a deluge his way. The cave was sloped and he had slipped deeper into the darkness. There was a flash of lightning and he glanced up at the opening. It didn't seem far and he began to climb towards it on his hands and knees.

There was another flash of lightning and a clap of thunder. The floor was slippery. He crawled through a river of mud and debris. He felt the wind driving as he neared the entrance. More lightning and thunder, the rain began to pelt the outside rock face with hurricane force winds. Randall heard a rumble.

"That's not lightning," he said.

The rumble got louder. The river turned violent as the cliff face melted into a mudslide. Chunks of rock and sand poured through the entrance, torrential rain and wind pushing it from behind. Lightning cracked and Randall lost his footing. He slid down on his stomach, past where he had been sleeping. The slope of the cave increased. He turned over, seeing rocks and debris bouncing ahead of him. Water splashed around him, abrasive mud tore at his back like sandpaper. Sliding deeper into the cave he was engulfed in darkness.

He tried to steady his breath, water rushing up his nose, forcing him to sneeze. He felt dizzy, vertigo churning in his stomach. He accelerated, dropping faster and faster towards an unknown fate. His entire effort was to stay focused in the moment. His survival counted on it.

33

Unable to see in the darkness, he tried to reach out with his other senses. He thought he heard water falling ahead. He kept looking for a place to get off this ride, a ledge or even a beach, but the slope went ever downward. His feet randomly met rock, the impact jarring him. The sound of tumbling stones was thunderous, assaulting his ears with bone crushing deafness. He could hear it front of him, plowing through the darkness. Behind him rocks tumbled in a race to push forward and hit him.

He screamed, yelling like a madman, shouting at the rock and mud. It made him feel good, a kia that came from deep in his gut.

The tumbling changed pitch, less deep sounds, as if the orchestra of rocks silenced the tubas. He could distinguish a difference. A new fear struck him. What if the debris blocked the entrance and clogged other parts of the cave? Could he possibly find his way out in the darkness?

The bottom dropped from under him. He plunged an unknown distance into a deep pool of water. There were eddys and currents, hydraulics that fought to imprison him in the dark water. He was disoriented, tossed by the forces to the point where he couldn't tell up from down.

He grew calm, resisting the natural urge to take in a panic breath. In that calm, he regained his composure and understood that he was pointed upright. He kicked, his legs propelling him upward. His hand finally broke the surface and he clawed the air above. He breathed deep, choking, his lungs taking in small gulps of water.

Kicking, fighting for his life, he began to swallow more water. It was getting difficult for him. His legs felt like rubber, useless. His hands refused to form cups that would help him swim. His legs felt cold and numb, stumps that refused to obey his commands. He was caught in an underground river.

*The struggle is over*, he thought. His eyes closed and he saw colors, bright flashes of light. The current lifted him up and carried him away. He felt like he was in the arms of a Valkyrie or an angel. The sound of running water pounded in his ears as he swirled in the darkness and slowly lost consciousness.

# Chapter 6

## The Bunker

"Where is Philippe?" asked Caroline. "What's taking him so long? This is my last day."

"I know," said Manny. "I called him over an hour ago. I'm about ready to close the place down anyway. Nobody has shown up, and there's nobody on the beach."

"It looks bleak out there," she said.

He moved in close to her. "It wasn't bleak when I made plans."

"I don't know if the weather will hold," she said. "Look out there. See on the horizon? There's dark clouds."

"Rain on your last day?" he said. "I won't allow it."

She laughed. "What did you have in mind?"

"I reserved a boat. I wanted to take you to a private island for a picnic," he said.

"Sounds romantic," she said, moving her lips close enough to kiss.

They were interrupted by a loud klaxon followed by an old time air raid siren.

"What now?" she said, irritated.

Manny got off his stool and went behind the bar. He began to store bottles and appliances in cabinets, clearing the counters.

"What's going on?" she asked.

"Emergency of some kind," he said. "I have to secure the bar and report."

"Can I help?" she asked.

He passed her a square plastic bin. "Gather up the condiments and things on the tables and put them in here." He finished clearing the bar. Caroline helped him gather chairs and stack them in corners along with tables.

There was a gust of wind and a cabinet door flew open crashing against the bar. Manny quickly secured it, placing wooden braces to latch it closed. He went to the open areas and started closing shutters and locking windows. The wind gusted again and he fought to control a shutter as it shook in his hand.

"This doesn't look good," she said.

"The bar is secure," he said. "We have to go now."

"Where?" she asked.

"Emergency operations center. There's a shelter there. The warning signal tells everyone in the village to go to their stations and assigned shelters. Let's go. It's not far."

Outside the sky was dark and they felt the full force of the wind. It was gusting, staying consistently strong as it pushed them sideways. The klaxon sounded again, longer this time, followed by the air raid siren. Rain came in spurts, hard and fast, beating them forward. Caroline slipped and fell off the walkway, the wind throwing her around like a damp rag. Manny sprung into action, a Galahad helping his lady in distress.

"You're fine," he said, gently pulling her to her feet. His voice was calm and reassuring. "I've got you." Gripping her tightly, their heads down from the wind and rain, he guided her to the emergency operations center, a large fortified building. It was a blockhouse, windowless, the walls sloped and built to withstand a tsunami. They went down a concrete corridor, entering the main building through a large metal door.

They were dripping wet and he brought her to a room just inside the entrance. There was a cart full of towels and he took one and gave it to her. "You're wearing a bathing suit, designed to get wet. I, on the other hand, need a change of clothes." He grabbed a towel and began drying.

"What is this place?" she asked. "It's like a big locker room."

"Exactly," he said. He brought her to a walk in closet. "This is where we store spare clothes. They're not fancy, but they're warm and dry. Pick something out."

She had no trouble searching. The clothes were organized and separated by size markers and she quickly found what she needed. A pair of warm leggings and a tunic length top that had plenty of pockets.

He looked handsome in the clothes he had chosen, dark trousers and a white shirt. The only thing missing was the bow tie to complete a dashing, magazine-perfect look. His bright teeth shone between smiling lips. She went up and hugged him. "Thank you for rescuing me back there," she said.

"I would never leave you lying in the dirt," he said.

"Then I'm a lucky woman." They drew closer. Someone came into the room and he quickly let her go. She watched him blush, the white knight turning red.

"Manny!" said Juliana. "Sorry to interrupt. But it's good to see you. Are you ready for this?"

"What's the emergency?" he asked.

"Let's find out," she said, leading them out of the locker room. "I think it has something to do with the bad weather we're having."

Manny turned to Caroline. "Well, you wanted to do something special on your last day," he said. "This should be interesting."

They followed Juliana through aisles bordered with cubicles. They were labeled with placards: Logistics, Operations, Power, Human Services, and so on. He led her to the far corner of the building to an area labeled "Information and Planning." It was warm and inviting, workstations on three sides and open on the other side to a large meeting area.

"This is where I work," he said.

"What do you do?" she asked.

"I manage this department," he said. "We report directly to the Think Tank who sits over there."

He pointed towards the meeting area at a large polished table. Behind it banks of wall mounted monitors displayed images and information. Juliana went to an assigned seat at the table, closed her eyes and slipped into a deep trance.

Manny took Caroline to stairs that led to an elevated gallery of seats overlooking the whole operation. "Guests usually sit up there," he said. She smiled, ascending the steps regally. There were comfortable lounge seats, small tables beside them.

She watched him open up two workstations, inputting on one, then the other. He went back and forth, stopping only to make or take a telephone call. Even then his ability to multitask was amazing, but that's what bartenders do anyway.

A few more people arrived and he immediately set them to task. Looking out over the sea of cubicles she could see everyone in the building was busy except her.

She turned her attention to the wall monitors watching images flash and cycle. One showed the sister city, "New Maya City of Worlds." Images of the jungle city flashed by: walkways and dwellings suspended from tall trees, stone and wood structures at ground level, pyramids and temples bordering a public forum. By the looks of things, they weren't having any weather problems.

She studied a display of current weather data telling her that the wind outside was gusting above seventy five miles per hour. No wonder they had trouble walking. Coastal flooding was already reported at three feet and rising. She caught a glimpse of Manny's bar on one of the monitors. The surf had eaten away at the beach and waves were clawing their way towards the shack. On other monitors wind was pushing palm trees over, forcing them to bend. A loose cabana chair tumbled across one screen. Boats in the marina tugged at their moorings, the floating dock undulating with the waves.

The reason for the emergency became clear to her as she spied a radar image. A hurricane, small and tight, with deadly force winds, was displayed on a weather map. A cone representing the projected path engulfed the Eighth Day Village of the Sun and spread deep into Mexico.

Through all this Juliana sat calmly at the table. Caroline wondered how she stayed focused with all the noise and activity going on around her.

A trim gentleman arrived, dark hair and tight trousers. He saw Caroline in the balcony and came up and introduced himself. "I wasn't aware we had observers. I'm Dr. Stine," he said. "Geneticist, scientist, and member of the Think Tank."

"Caroline Garman," she answered. "Think Tank? What exactly is that?"

"A loose group. We are made up of people with diverse talents. We come up with ideas and solutions that help the village and the surrounding environment."

"You have your work cut out for you now."

"Yes," he said. "A hurricane. Very mysterious. Usually we see them coming days in advance."

"I know," she said. "I'm a meteorologist."

He smiled. "Then what are you doing up in the observation gallery? Come down and join the Think Tank."

"Me?" she asked.

"Yes," he urged. "We need your expertise."

He escorted her to the conference table below where he pulled a chair out for her. "Here you go. The computer is in the table," he explained. "See the monitor through the surface?"

"Yes," she said.

He pushed some buttons and a keyboard slid into view. He used it to log in, saying, "This should get you started."

Juliana was just emerging from her trance.

"You've met Juliana, our high priestess?" he asked.

Caroline nodded.

"I've been in direct contact with Gaia," she said, her voice little more than a whisper.

"Juliana has the ability to communicate with everything from ascended masters to planetary consciousnesses," he said. "Her function here is to contact Gaia, the Earth spirit that is this planet. Her input has been very helpful in the past."

"Gaia is wounded," said Juliana. "This storm is not of her making. She is in pain and needs our help."

"We'll do what we can," said Stine. "Let Gaia know that."

Juliana closed her eyes. "The storm is unstoppable. What has begun must end. Time is of the essence. We work together to restore balance."

"Gaia has spoken," said Stine.

"So I hear," said Darius, arriving on the tail end of the conversation. "Juliana is powerful." He scanned the area. "Where is everybody? Randall? Barclay? I would at least expect Cameron to astral project. He never misses a meeting."

"I'm afraid we're it, Darius," said Stine.

"Who is she?" asked Darius, indicating Caroline.

Stine made introductions. "Darius, this is Caroline Garmin. Doctor Darius is another member of the Think Tank."

She stood up and faced him. "Pleased," she said.

He spoke to Stine. "What is she doing here?"

"Subject matter expert," said Stine. "She may have the answers, or at least contribute to them."

"Where did you find her?" asked Darius.

"In the gallery," said Stine. "Amazing, right?"

Darius frowned.

Caroline cleared her throat. "Do you want me to go back up in the gallery?"

Darius answered yes while Stine said no.

"I'd like to help," she said. "You're short handed. Everyone else in this bunker is busy, and frankly you need all the help you can get."

"We'll see about that," said Darius. He looked about again. "Where is everybody?"

Caroline turned to Stine. "Thank you for your invitation, Dr. Stine. I'll continue with my analysis now," she said flatly. She went back to her seat, then looked up at Darius, slight irritation in her voice. "Oh, and to answer your questions, Darius. Randall took off heading south this morning with Anji. He said he was going exploring today. Barclay McKenner and Franklin Van Dorn went out to sea to commune with dolphins. They're likely lost out there. I suggest we launch a search and rescue team to find them as soon as the weather clears. And Singh? He went out into the jungle in an air car, somewhere east of here. Said he had to answer the call of his soul. Something he had to recover. Mysterious fellow. Wind and rain bands haven't reached him, but they will soon. I suggest someone try to communicate with him and let him know there's a storm headed his way. It would give him a chance to find shelter before getting caught in the open." She smiled. "Any more questions, *Doctor*?"

"What about Ravi?" asked Darius. "Randall's faithful manservant and friend. He's a member of the Think Tank."

Manny overheard and approached the table. "Ravi went out on horseback looking for Randall at the first sign of trouble. When the wind picked up and the surf got angry he turned back. Fortunately he hadn't gone far. He said he was more concerned for the horse's safety than his own."

"Good old Ravi," said Darius.

"He checked into shelter A4 a short time ago," said Manny.

"I guess that's roll call," said Darius. "You better stay at the table with us, Manny."

"My place is in Information and Planning," he said.

"Not for this incident," said Darius. "Too many vacancies in the Think Tank. It's time to step up. We need you."

Darius looked into their faces and found agreement. Juliana smiled, Stine nodded, and Caroline looked at him like there was no question about it. "Very well then," he said. "We are the Think Tank. Let's get down to business."

"You know, we've been trying to recruit you into the Think Tank for years now, Manny," said Stine.

"I'm happy bartending," he said.

"Yes," said Stine. "Where you hope to meet the next Mrs. Manny DuBois."

Caroline looked up and smiled from across the table, then stared back into the computer screen. "The hurricane has intensified," she said. "Winds are clocking over a hundred miles per hour consistently. I've never seen a storm intensify this quickly."

"I ran several models on the GIS workstation," said Manny.

"The maps on the wall monitor?" she asked, surprised. "That's your work?"

Manny grinned. "The model uses historical data to project best guess scenarios, but I have never seen anything like this either. There has never been an event like this in the past, hence no history."

"It appeared so sudden," said Caroline. "The forecast for today was clear skies and calm seas."

"Gaia says it is not natural, not of her making," said Juliana.

"I concur with that," said Caroline.

"If it's not natural then what else can it be?" asked Manny.

"Only one other choice," said Caroline. "It's man made."

"How is that possible?" asked Darius.

"It's possible," said Stine.

"Man made? How can that be?" Darius stood up and faced the monitors. He fought against worry and fear, thinking about what Randall would do in the face of this. He stared into the screens for a while as if they were crystal balls. He was not trying to see the future, it was the present that interested him. Mathematical formulas churned in his head as he observed and calculated the things familiar to engineers: forces, resistance, material strength, hydraulics, projected casualties.

"The Think Tank is at half strength while the hurricane is at full strength," he said. "This is a  formula for disaster any way you look at it."

# Chapter 7

## Lost at Sea

Franklin Van Dorn tried to stay under the waves. Currents of water still pushed him around, but with his rebreather on, it was less effort than bobbing helplessly on the surface. He was extremely disoriented, lost in a world of visual and audio distortion. All he could think about was survival. As he floated in the water he prayed, not only for his own safety, but for the life and safety of his friend as well. *If only Barclay were here. With two people we would double our chance for survival. With two people there is encouragement and hope.*

Above him was darkness, the shadow of purple clouds obscuring the sky. Below him lay the darkness of the depths. The body compresses as you go deeper. At one point it reaches a density that makes it sink rather than float. It was one of his fears. With no way of knowing his depth except a feeling, Franklin Van Dorn was truly lost in an abyss.

He felt the pressure build up in his ears, knowing he was sinking deeper. Desperately he clawed for the surface, only to come up through the waves and be tossed about like a kid's pool toy. Currents spun him in circles. There was a bright flash up above and he sunk beneath the waves again into the relative comfort of the dark and turbulent sea.

Flashes of lightning continued above him. Was it above him? Like someone locked in a sensory deprivation tank, after a while Franklin's mind began to slip. Some kind of rapture of the deep. *Am I in a photo shoot?* he thought. *Lights keep flashing all around me. Pose for the cameras. Now, where is that fake dolphin prop?* Adrift in a world he could not process, there came a flash of light that did not go away. It called to him like the light at the end of a tunnel, a threshold that, should he cross it, would become permanent. He looked about thinking, *where are my loved ones to greet me at death? Do I not have any friends?*

He swam upward and broke through the surface to calm seas and bright daylight. His ears popped and he spun around looking in all directions.

He took the rebreather out of his mouth, his jaw sore and aching. He realized he had been biting down on it, a sign of his anxiety and fear. He breathed in the fresh air, wondering if there were any truth to his words as he asked the question, "Am I dead?"

He spun around, looking in every direction. He was near a wall of water, a fantastic cloud of rain moving sideways and upwards. He could hear wind slicing the air, creating strange sounds. He heard freight trains passing close by, the cries of lost and dying souls, and the rhythmic pounding of slow, steady jackhammers. The wall was approaching him fast, the sound of the wind beginning to hurt his ears. He could feel an updraft, a current of water being lifted from the surface as it pulled him towards it. He felt like he would be sucked up into oblivion if he got any closer.

Dead or not it was terrifying to him, feeding the illusion that his life was over and he existed in some kind of altered reality. Above he saw sunlight but in the wall of water he saw fear and darkness. It kicked off something in him, the natural response to fight or flee. Adrenaline surged in his system and he swam away from the wall as hard as he could.

Despite the calm water he grew tired after a while. His arms ached and he turned on his back, continuing to kick with his feet. He heard birds overhead, seagulls screeching. Some were resting on the surface near him. It was a strange sight. *Why are things so calm? I must be dead. What is this place?*

He felt the current around him, a slight eddy that made him rotate. He turned vertical in the water, looking around to see, his head turning back and forth. It was distant, but he noticed the deadly wall of water surrounding him completely, visible in all directions. *The borders of hell,* He thought.

The current began to swirl. *Am I in a whirlpool? No, I'm a bug in the bathtub. Away those troubles down the drain. Ha ha!*

And in madness there is truth as he thought. *Look at me. I'm the eye of the storm.*

∂∞

In another part of the ocean, Barclay McKenner hid in darkness beneath a capsized boat holding on to a broken piece of rub rail. He jerked up and down with the waves, hitting his head occasionally. He was definitely not in the calm eye of the storm. This was an angry ocean.

"You're in trouble, Barclay. This is not a good place to be," he said.

A wave hit the side of the boat causing it to pitch. He covered his head, worried about hitting something solid again. Outside the wind howled, the waves crashed against the boat, but inside was almost like a protective cave. It was an illusion of safety.

"Nope, can't stay here," he said, the echo of his voice coming back hollow and empty as it bounced off the insides of the boat. He looked up at the radio microphone dangling above him. If only he could call for help. And what would they do? Still, he had heard about the Coast Guard risking their lives in daring rescues to save others.

"I'm in trouble," he said. "Gotta think."

Waves beat against the hull, washing over the upside down boat, slapping it around with loud thumps. Barclay continued to talk over the sound. "I have my rebreather on, but where to go? They say it's easier for the rescue teams to find you if you stay with the boat."

There was another thump against the hull.

"That didn't sound like a wave," he said. "A heavy object maybe."

And yet another thump, then a thump against his thigh as he was rammed by something. He dipped his head below the surface, breathing through his apparatus. It was Neptune, one of his dolphin friends.

*Oh my God*, he thought. *You heard my cry for help. You've come back for me.* He projected love at the dolphin, thanks and gratitude. From his motions Barclay knew he wanted to take him somewhere. Grabbing the dorsal fin, he held on as best he could. Neptune took one more deep breath, squeaking frantically before pulling him under, descending into the depths.

Barclay could only hang on.

# Chapter 8

## The Life Council

Randall slowly became conscious of his surroundings. He was in a green, brightly lit room, the walls seemingly radiating life. His vision was blurry and he stared at the bright lights, wondering if they would blind him. Instead he felt a wave of calm come over him as the weariness left his eyes. The bright lights came into focus, turning into three beings seated behind a table on the other side of the room.

"Are you comfortable?" one of them asked.

"Where am I?" asked Randall.

"This is the world between worlds," said the being. "Your spirit guides are here also." Randall turned to the right, becoming aware of a rather large group standing nonchalantly nearby. Most were smiling and laughing, love pouring out of them. A few were serious, their look sharply focused on him. He turned back towards the table, his eyes squinting.

"Perhaps we should lower our level of vibration," said one of the beings.

"Yes," said another.

It was as if the lights flickered in a lightning storm. The beings came into sharp focus, the light that they were emitting receded into their heads and hearts where a glow still radiated. Like a particle of dust in the sunlight he was caught up in the bright beams that radiated from their centers.

"We are your life council," said the one in the middle.

"What's that mean?" asked Randall.

"You don't remember us," said the being on the left. "We were here with you when you planned this life."

There were murmurs and agreement from the spirit guides.

"You mean, it's over?" asked Randall.

"Step through the door on the left and you will lose the connection." As if on command, a door appeared on his left, forming itself out of the smooth, green wall. He looked down at his navel, seeing a silver cord coming out of it. It twisted and curved showing small, dull blobs of light moving slowly inside it as it dropped through the floor and out of sight.

"Life has been hard for you," he continued. "You have toiled all the days of your life. Are you ready to rest?"

"Rest?" said Randall. "That's for the weary. I fight old age, and it wins some days, but I still find joy in that struggle."

"You find joy many places, Baba," said the being on the right.

"Is that not what living is for?"

There was a snicker from the peanut gallery of spirit guides.

"Then is it life you choose?"

"There is so much left to do," said Randall. "Service to humanity seems an endless task, but it is a labor of love."

"That it is," said the being in the center.

The door on the left opened and another bright entity moved into the room. He didn't quite walk, at least that was not what you would call it. More like gliding. He went over to the table and spoke to the beings at the table. When he was finished he turned and looked towards Randall. A more piercing gaze there never was. Twin beams of energy came from his eyes, dissecting every aspect of Randall's life. When he was finished he smiled and left the room through the same door he entered.

"Ah," said the being at the center of the table. "The Lords of Karma have spoken. This was not of your doing. It is an available exit point, however, should you choose to move on."

50

"I don't understand," said Randall.

"Do you wish to go on living?" asked the being.

"Of course," said Randall. "I choose life."

"So be it," said the being. The room seemed to fade like light before dusk. As Randall lost consciousness again he thought he heard laughter and applause from the peanut gallery.

∂∞

"Where am I?" asked Randall.

"You're in a hospital. Lie still, you're being treated."

"No, I meant *where* am I?"

"Be silent. I'll be done shortly."

Randall heard high frequency noises, buzzing like bees on amphetamines. He felt sensations within him making him squirm. His skin itched.

"Will he be okay, doctor?" said another voice.

"He will be if he lies still and stops fidgeting."

Randall did his best to obey. "I'm alive," he said.

"Of course you are," said the doctor. "Otherwise I would be wasting my time."

He felt his breath, the precious giver of life. He began to breathe rhythmically, putting himself in a meditative state. Using self hypnosis techniques, he alienated himself from his body, adrift in a sea of love. His mind turned towards healing as it gathered reiki and divine energy and channeled it into his body.

"That's more like it," said the doctor. He continued his work for some time. Machines hummed. Randall inhaled, assaulted by the scent of medicinal herbs and balms. The doctor continued to scan and probe Randall looking for signs of injury. "Since you're conscious, let me explain what happened to you. These two gentlemen saw you floating near death in the river. They pulled you out of a fast moving current and brought you here. We'd like to know how you got there in the first place."

Randall was quiet, still drifting. He focused, bringing himself back to reality.

"It's okay," said the doctor. "You can talk now. To begin with, what is your name?"

"Randall."

"How do you feel, Randall?"

"Better than I should, I gather. I've been unconscious, you say. How did I get here?"

"You were brought here for treatment because of your injuries."

"Where is here?" asked Randall. "What place is this?"

"A hospital," said the doctor.

"No," said Randall. "What city is this?"

The doctor thought it a strange question, but he answered anyway. "Tobit," he said, beginning to check Randall for signs of brain injury.

"Never heard of it," said Randall.

"Where are you from, then?" asked the doctor.

"Eighth Day Village of the Sun."

"Never heard of it."

"How about New Maya City of Worlds?" asked Randall. "Ever hear of that?"

"Never. But I like the name," said the doctor. "Where is it?"

"Mexico."

The two other men in the room looked at each other, their eyes full of questions.

The doctor gave them a quick glance and a nod, turning his attention back to Randall. "Mexico. Now that's a place I've heard of," he said. "Good spot for a holiday. Tell me again what happened to you, Randall. Whatever you can remember."

He groped through the fog in his brain. "I remember a storm," he said. "I was trapped on the beach, waves pushing me against the rocks. I saw a cave and climbed up to it to get to safety. I was tired and I slept once I got inside the cave. Rain and mud poured through the entrance like a river." He stopped talking, his mind groping for what happened next.

"Go on with your story," said the doctor.

Randall struggled. "The water came. I lost my footing and slid deeper in the cave, deep into the Earth." he paused again. "Well below sea level, I imagine."

"Go on," said the doctor.

"It was like going down a water slide," he said.

"A water slide through hell, I imagine," said the doctor. "You have abrasions, a broken femur, and sub dermal trauma. I am using accelerated field growth to repair the broken parts. The skin abrasions will take longer."

"That's modern medicine," said Randall. "You can make a bone heal long before a man's outer hide gets fixed."

"You have a sense of humor, Randall. Definitely a sign you are on the mend. Your story makes sense and it is consistent with your injuries."

"I wouldn't lie to you," said Randall. "You're my doctor, aren't you?"

The doctor laughed. "Yes, I am your doctor."

"Where did you say I am?" he asked. "Tobit?"

The doctor smiled. "You've had a serious injury. You were unconscious. Give yourself time to recover. And keep that thigh bone as still as possible. The itch will go away soon but the field must remain active a little while longer. Here, I'll give you something to help you sleep."

The doctor went to a wall panel and logged in, spoke his prescription into the microphone. "Play program theta sleep three. Adjust frequency and room lighting to match the patient's aura. Initiate."

A high frequency pitch sounded and the lights in the room dimmed to green.

"Green again?" said Randall, closing his eyes into darkness.

"Rest now, and I will be back to check on you later." The doctor turned away from him, moving to the two gentlemen by the door. "He'll be okay, I repaired most of the damage. He just needs rest. Now let's get out of here or we'll all be sleeping on the floor."

Once out in the hall, he asked them to come to his office. There, the doctor offered them drinks and refreshment from a small refrigerator. "You did a good thing today," he said. "You saved a life. Can I get your names for the record?"

"I'm Justice Hansen, and this is Praetor John."

"You live in Tobit?" asked the doctor.

"In the park district," said Praetor. "That's where we found him, not far from where the cave spring feeds the Tobit river."

"Interesting," said the doctor.

"What was he talking about?" asked Justice. "Someplace called Mexico?"

"I've heard of it," said the doctor.

"He is definitely not from our city," said Praetor.

"No, he's not," said the doctor. "You must remain quiet about this for now. I need more time to question him and gather facts. If you give me your contact information I will update you. Otherwise, if you wish to remain anonymous, I will respect that too."

"No," said Justice. "I want to know about him."

"Me to," said Praetor.

"Okay, I'll be in touch when I know more. Thank you for your cooperation. You can go now. I'm going to go back and look in on our patient again."

They left the office and went their different ways. The doctor found Randall asleep. The program automatically shut itself off when it sensed his deep sleep. He checked the femur one more time. It was regenerating and the patient was healing well.

He left the room and walked up two flights of stairs to the director's office. His message was simple. "I have something to report, sir. Another outworlder. He's downstairs now healing from traumatic injuries."

"You should have let him die," said the director.

"You don't mean that," said the doctor.

The director looked away. "No, I don't," he said. "It just seems kinder at times. Our ways are different than the surface dwellers. I don't see them adjust very often. Some try to get back to the surface, some become lugubrious and lose heart, and there are those who commit suicide. Only a rare few make the adjustment. The few that do manage to get back to the surface spread rumors and create legends that invite more of the curious. Why do we bother?"

"Our people are Xenophobic," said the doctor. "That much is true. We have not had much success with the surface people."

"Why did you treat this man then?"

"I thought he was one of our own, sir. His aura was bright. He was unconscious when he was brought in. I had no choice but to treat him."

"Yes, yes," said the director. "You have done well. I'll notify the authorities. He'll have to get used to being here, just like the others who find their way down here. We have no choice but to keep him here now."

# Chapter 9

## Singh Song

Cameron Singh finished a last bite of one of Manny's sandwiches, a tofu delight seasoned with microgreens. He loaded the rest of the provisions in his backpack which contained all his instruments and tools. Taking a drink from his canteen he strapped it to the outside and hoisted the pack on his back. The air car rested gently on the ground. It was essentially a giant personal drone, fan blades positioned for optimum maneuverability. The wind had come up suddenly making it challenging to operate. After being pushed towards rocks and treetops several times, he decided to land. Using instinct over intellect, he chose this spot on the edge of a wide meadow where the trees and foliage provided some protection from the wind.

Where it was, he could not say, except that he was in the middle of unexplored jungle. At least, unexplored to him. He took some readings, but without accurate ground data or imagery they were useless. For some unexplained reason the GPS satellites refused to lock in and the needle of his pocket compass spun in circles.

The jungle had a familiar feel to it, a smell that seemed to trigger memories. He had spent an incarnation as an Aztec, a lifetime he was having trouble remembering. It would take time to research, but he could use his talents and look into it. All he had to do was visit the library of his past, a higher dimensional storehouse that he had access to. It would then be a matter of finding the right volume of that past life and carefully accessing it. Problem was, they were not always filed in chronological order as some earth bound souls might like it to be. Instead they were organized by experience, lessons learned, ties to other beings, and other odd cross references that, he assumed, made more sense in a higher dimensional realm. In this case, he was having trouble knowing where to begin. Thus, this expedition.

He breathed deep. There was definitely a feeling about this place, but where to start from here? Which direction?

He scanned the area. Dense jungle rimmed the edges of the meadow, an impassible wall of vegetation. There was a small pond on the other side. Animals gently sipped from it. He started walking towards it.

"Where there are animals there are animal trails," he said.

He heard a voice behind him. "Be careful, my friend. You would not want to walk up on a jaguar."

Singh turned around and saw nothing. The meadow behind him was empty except for the air car. "Who said that?"

"I did," he heard.

He turned around, again, nothing. There was a gust of wind and an uneasy feeling settled in his gut. The sky was unusually dark. Rain clouds can gather over the jungle and let loose every afternoon, but it was early morning and the forecast for today had been clear skies, even this far inland. Despite the prediction, ominous, dark clouds were quickly moving into view. He was having second thoughts about this expedition.

The animals around the pond became alert. A deer leapt away into the jungle, monkeys took to the trees, and it became quiet. Rain began to fall, gentle at first, then with increasing strength.

"Better get a move on," said the voice. "It's not far."

"I'm not going anywhere until you tell me who you are," he shouted.

"Ixpetz."

"Are you a negative entity?"

"No," came the voice. "I am you."

"How can you be me? I would know about you from my past."

"Of course you would," said Ixpetz. "That's why our soul decided it should be this way. The same way human incarnations receive a mind wipe, you have been blocked from knowledge of me. I'm afraid we will have to use old fashioned communication like talking."

"But why?"

"Perhaps God loves a mystery as much as you do. Sometimes, knowing everything can be boring. We better hurry, though. Unlike you, I have been granted the ability to see the immediate future clearly. The probabilities change by the moment. Your chance of finding shelter are decreasing the more you dawdle here."

"Why don't I just get in the air car and fly home?"

"Because of this."

The wind gusted. Lightning crackled and struck a tree near the air car. A branch fell, smashing the front of it. Monkeys scattered, their screeching making him jump.

He saw Ixpetz across the clearing, a glowing image similar to his own when he astral projected. "This way," called Ixpetz. "Quickly. I can get you there safely if you hurry."

There was another flash of lightning followed by a roar of thunder. Singh needed no more motivation. He ran towards the glowing image, thinking how Ixpetz was him. This was a new experience. His mind explored the possibilities as he raced down the trail that led away from the meadow. Again there was a familiar feeling to it. The thunder jarred his senses. He looked behind, thinking he might see a man dressed in battle armor following him, trying to swipe at him with a machete or a sword or something. He could almost hear the clanking metal.

He thought it was a trick of his mind. Of course he would run harder and faster if someone was chasing him. He lost his concentration, not paying attention to the path ahead. It ended in a stone wall where he came to a sudden halt. The narrow path turned both left and right as it followed the wall. He chose right. Water dripped on him from the jungle leaves as they caught and channeled the rain from overhead. He felt a chill and he came to the end of the wall. The path split, one going straight ahead, a narrower, less traveled trail heading left. He pushed branches aside, took a few steps and realized he had turned a corner and found a continuation of the wall. He stumbled forward until he came to another corner, the truth dawning on him. This was not a wall, but a building. He followed this edge until he turned a third corner going almost completely around the building. He rubbed his eyes, water still dripping around him. His arms disturbed jungle leaves that were cupped and pointed upward. They retaliated by dousing him in water. He tried to stay focused and mindful of the environment. What was he supposed to find here?

He tripped over something, rocks in the path. His hand reached out to the wall for balance. He stumbled forward landing on his face. He laid there for a minute feeling the pain. An astral body wouldn't hurt like this. He spit the detritus from his mouth, bits of rotting leaf and dirt that got caught up in it when he fell. His face was peppered with mud. Mustering his strength, he stood up against the heavy rain, welcoming it this time as he allowed it to fill his mouth and clean it.

He spit the water out, brushed away mud from his eyes, face, and chest. He cupped his hands, catching water and washing some more.

"Are you finished?" It was Ixpetz leaning back patiently against the wall. "If you had turned the other way when you first got here, you would have found the entrance quicker."

"Here?" asked Singh. "This is the entrance?"

"Are you blind? What did you just trip over?"

Singh looked down, got back on his knees and cleared away dirt and debris. It was a run of stones, raised off the jungle floor slightly at a ninety degree angle to the building. He cleared more away, noticing a parallel run a short distance away.

"You'll have to dig," said Ixpetz. "Time and the jungle have not been good to this place."

Singh slid his backpack off, unpacked a collapsible shovel and began to dig between the raised sections. Not far from the surface he struck stone. Working still, water dripping off and around him, he dug until he had cleared away a set of stairs. They were shallow, leading to a hole framed with heavy stone slabs. It was not long before he had the debris and the entrance clean enough to expose a narrow hole he might be able to squeeze through. Wind gusted above him. Trees shook and leaves fell. He might have to dig himself back out. And wouldn't this hole capture water and funnel it through the entrance. This could be a trap that could drown him.

"Old fashioned fear," he said out loud. "When the soul is the warrior there is nothing to fear."

The storm provided him with yet another mystery as he probed past the fear. The report he read before he left this morning said fair weather. Now this. "Maybe this is a psychic storm," he said. "Imaginary, or occurring on a higher dimension. The air car was wrecked right on cue. My past self appears, helping me with this mission. Finding this place so fast. What would Darius say? *Too many coincidences to be a coincidence.*"

Lightning crackled, water poured down the exposed steps. "Do I accept this reality?" Water pelted his skin. He tasted it in his mouth, the slight flavor of raw plants as he opened his mouth to catch the stream of water falling off a leaf. He felt the dirt against his skin. Years, no centuries, lifetimes of navigating higher realms, he had experienced things just as real. "Is this real?"

"You're thinking too much," said Ixpetz.

He dug deeper with the shovel revealing a trough, part of the design to take water away from the entrance. He cleaned the drain and the water began to flow out from around his feet.

Lightning again. The rain had created a river, most of it moving away from the entrance but enough to make him uncomfortable. He needed shelter. Breaking out his flashlight, he aimed the beam down the hole, looking for lizards and snakes. Who knows what took up refuge behind these walls. Bugs he could deal with. Scorpions and snakes he'd rather not.

Shaking away his fears, he put his shovel through the hole and began to crawl into the tight stone corridor.

# Chapter 10

## Look Me in the Eye

"Winds outside are a sustained hundred and forty miles per hour," said Caroline. "It's officially a class four hurricane."

"The eye is approaching quickly, too" said Stine. "Less than an hour and a half away by my estimates."

"What could have caused this?" asked Darius.

"I'm still working on that," said Caroline.

"If we knew what caused it we might have a clue about how to stop it," said Manny.

"You don't stop a hurricane," said Darius.

"Why not?" asked Manny. "We've stopped a tsunami before. We even harvested its energy."

Caroline turned, her mouth half open. "This is the first I've heard of this. I'd like to hear some details please."

"Maybe later," said Manny. He turned to Darius. "You still haven't given me an answer, Darius. Why can't we stop a hurricane?"

"Stopping the hurricane is not our emergency plan," said Darius flatly.

"True. Our strategy for a hurricane has always been to assemble in shelters and ride it out," said Stine. "We built the village with safety in mind, planning on all contingencies. We can withstand floods and a storm surge up to fifteen feet."

"This village may be safe," said Caroline. "But what about the rest of the towns and villages in its path?" She pointed to the monitor. "A category four hurricane is not going to play itself out easily over land.

It's going to tear up the countryside, cause flood and tornado damage, and displace countless people. If you have the ability to stop that, then why not?"

"What makes you think we can do anything besides wait in shelters?" asked Darius.

"What about the Long Range Acoustical Device?" asked Manny. "It worked on the tsunami."

"In this wind it would be ripped off the pedestal the moment we deployed it," said Darius.

"You could try it during the eye of the storm," said Caroline. In a quiet voice she added, "It's headed right for us."

After some silence, Juliana said, "Is there a way we can keep the storm centered over the village until it blows out?"

"Keep it here?" asked Stine. "Are you crazy?"

"If we keep the storm stationary somehow, we would stop it from moving further inland. Once over land, they tend to blow out. That's another way we could save a lot of people a lot of suffering. Isn't that what this village is about?"

Manny sat there deep in thought. He was staring into a bottle of water, playing with it, watching the water swirl inside the half empty bottle. He thought about how he watched water go down the drain countless times, swirling and sucking air as it emptied. He always had fun playing with the tornado spout as a kid in the bathtub.

Storms are magical, he thought. They carry massive energy. They purge the land of rot using wind and rain, making way for change and for new things. In the great oceans, birds and insects travel in the eye, migrating from island to island and even between continents. In the aftermath, people are united by the tragedy. For some, it is the only way they ever come to know their neighbors and their community.

"I still can't figure it out," said Caroline. "Perfect weather predicted this morning. High pressure, no precipitation, then a tropical storm just materialized out of nowhere."

"You all keep asking what caused it," said Juliana. "I think a better question is who caused it."

"Let's continue to think positively," said Manny. "We are sheltered and our chances for survival are high. We can rebuild anything, and when we do it's always smarter, safer, and stronger. People, our most precious resource, are protected. Why not try something new in addition to everything we normally do?"

"I don't see why not," said Stine.

"Gaia would agree," said Juliana.

Darius turned to Caroline. "Do you have a vote in this?"

"I don't like hurricanes," she said. "I like the idea of fighting back for a change"

"It seems we have three choices here," said Manny. "Wait it out until the storm passes, which is what we usually do. We could somehow hold it in place over our village and it keep here until it blows itself out. Or the last option, blow it out ourselves."

"Nice, Manny," said Darius. "Just like a birthday candle."

"That's an interesting idea," said Caroline.

"It would take a hell of a breath," said Stine.

"I propose we pursue all three options," said Manny.

"I second that," said Stine.

"Okay, said Darius. "We don't need to do anything about option one, so lets think about the other two."

"What about you, Juliana," asked Manny. "Has Gaia given us any clues on what we can do?"

"She is in pain and keeps repeating 'Restore the balance' over and over."

"Great, how do we do that?" asked Stine.

"Scientists have been studying hurricanes for centuries," said Caroline. "They haven't come up with any way of stopping them so far. This is new territory."

"Let's be optimistic, shall we?" said Stine. "We're the Think Tank after all. We think out of the box."

"Why don't we erect a giant wall? When the wind hits it, it will stop," said Juliana.

"We don't have time to build a wall that tall," said Caroline. "It would have to be five or ten miles high, and that may not be tall enough. What makes you think it would hold up? Besides, the wind would accelerate when it hit the wall. That's what it does when it comes to mountains. The wind cycles violently causing updrafts and tornadoes in the process."

"We weren't actually going to build a wall," said Stine. "We can use the force field technology licensed to us by the extraterrestrials."

"Do you know how much energy that would take?" said Darius. "Using the equation force equals mass times acceleration, a hundred and forty mile an hour wind would generate well over five thousand newtons of force. We can't generate a force field with that amount of resistance." He pointed at Caroline. "She's right. The wall would crumble before we could deploy it."

"We could use every force field generator we have at once," said Manny. "Surely that's enough to tip the balance."

"I'm not so sure," said Darius. "Besides, you heard what she said about walls."

"It's going to be bad enough when it gets to the mountains behind the village," said Caroline. "A wall is not the answer."

"Maybe not," said Manny. He stopped spinning the water bottle and took a drink from it.

"So we can't really blow it out," said Darius. "What else have we got? How do we hold it in place and stop it from moving?"

"I've seen miracles here," said Caroline. "Hurricanes are attracted to low pressure areas. Do you have any way of generating a low pressure area?"

"How low?"

"Pretty low," she said. "Below 900 millibars at best guess. I'll have to monitor the storm and make some calculations to be exact," she said.

"It's an option to consider, although I can't think about how we'd do that off hand. But go ahead and proceed with your analysis and calculations." Darius turned towards the rest of the think tank. "What else have we got?" he asked.

"I keep thinking we should be able to destroy it," said Juliana. "Man created it, man should be able to destroy it."

"We're not sure of that," said Darius.

"What, that man created it? You can bet that it's not natural, Darius. Gaia already told us that."

"Who would create a storm like this?" asked Darius.

"And send it to our village?" asked Juliana. "Only one man with a reason and the money, and you've all met him."

A light came on inside Darius. "Harmon Rothschild," he said. "But why?"

"Revenge," she said. "He came here not long ago to steal our technology. He even brought a general with him in case he needed an army to take it forcefully. We thwarted his plan. We opened our minds and technology to help the world in the throes of economic disaster. We did it by creating independence and autonomy in villages and towns on every continent, experimental communities where people can choose to live a different lifestyle."

"Off the grid, they used to call it," said Caroline.

"Rothschild's empire is eroding and the world that he owned is slipping from his grasp," said Juliana. "He likely blames up for his problems."

"How could he cause such a hurricane, of all things?" asked Manny.

"You can buy anything if you have enough money," said Juliana. "Even a hurricane, I imagine."

"Where do you even shop for one?" asked Caroline.

"He must have some kind of weather control," said Darius. "If this storm is, as we concluded, man  made, then it must be possible somehow."

"I'll contact Carson, I mean President Whiteweather, and see if something like weather control even exists," said Juliana. "He would know." She picked up a handset and got up from her chair, wandering towards the gallery for some privacy.

"My course projections continually place the eye directly over the village," said Caroline.

"So?" asked Darius.

"We will have a short window of opportunity, a calm moment before the other side of the wall hits us with equal strength winds from the opposite direction. Whatever we're going to do, I suggest we do it while the eye is here."

"That's encouraging," said Stine.

"Hurricanes hate cold weather," said Darius. "Maybe we could freeze it."

Caroline laughed. "We could never do that." Her eyes suddenly lit up. "But even a temperature drop of a few degrees might make a difference."

"Our refrigeration and air conditioning experts might be able to come up with something," said Stine.

"If we act on any of these options, it's going to take a lot of power," said Darius. "I'm not sure we have the resources for more than one of these options."

Manny half heard the conversation as he continued to be lost inside the swirling bottle of water, thinking. "A force field might do it," he mumbled to himself.

Caroline heard him. "We already agreed it was a bad idea," she said. "Tornadoes and waterspouts, remember?"

"No, not on the side," said Manny. He spun the bottle and held it upside down, water swirling in a cyclone. He put his hand over it. "What if we deployed a force field on top?"

# Chapter 11

## Lights Under the Sea

Neptune plunged deeper. Barclay kept clearing his ears, holding his nose and pumping air into his inner ear as the pressure increased. Where was he taking him?

He trusted the dolphin. The first time he swam with a pod, Neptune singled him out. It was strange, but a friendship was formed, not one based on anything you could put your finger or fin on. In a quiet moment, Barclay McKenner looked into the eye of Neptune and saw the universe. One can only imagine what Neptune saw, but the two shared a psychic conversation that transcended species. McKenner, like Joan Ocean in Hawaii, had proven that dolphin were equal to humans and that each species could learn much from each other.

There were lights up ahead. Lights at the bottom of the sea. It appeared to be a platform in a bubble, or some such thing. There were objects on the platform, distorted in the water. He had trouble determining what they were. Neptune pulled him under the dome and brought him to an opening in the underside of the platform. There was air above and McKenner surfaced into a small pool. Neptune emerged next to him, flipping and chattering excitedly like dolphin do, then he turned on his side and splashed him with his fin. Barclay reached out and patted his friend on the belly, wondering if dolphin smile because of emotion or because their muscles and bones are shaped that way. A few more pats and Neptune chuckled, then turned and dove into the sea.

Barclay swam to the side of the pool and rolled onto the platform. It felt soft, like some kind of plastic. Water formed puddles around him and he stood up. He pulled the rebreather out of his mouth and took several deep breaths through his nose. The air was good, he felt energized by it. He squeezed the moisture out of his clothes, trying to force it back into the pool with his foot. He heard a voice in his head say, "You might need this."

Someone placed a towel in his hand, just what he needed. He wiped his face dry and turned to thank his benefactor.

The towel dropped to the floor beside him as he said, "Oh, my God!"

Barclay stared into the face of a gray being, looking like a large infant with an oversized head and disproportionate appendages.

The gray being did not speak. Instead there was a tall humanoid behind him, thin and wiry. He was wearing some kind of sparkling gown that flowed like wind rustling through tree leaves. "Don't be alarmed," he said. "He won't harm you. He just wants to help you."

"I'm not afraid," said Barclay, a little nervous. "Just amazed."

"You're from the Eighth Day Village of the Sun," said the humanoid.

"Yes," said Barclay. *Now how did you know that?*

"I can see it in your thoughts," said the humanoid, answering his unspoken words. "We have several agreements with your people, as we do with many governments. Your village is one of the few that allows us to test new devices. When we take on your form and walk among you there, nobody accosts us or otherwise disturbs our thoughts."

"It's why I live there, too," said Barclay.

"The exchange of technology has been beneficial for both of us. Also, there are resources here on Earth that are unavailable anywhere else in the galaxy."

"Like what?" asked Barclay.

"Minerals and such. There is a material we gather from a few feet below the surface. We use it to power our ships."

Barclay looked around. The dome formed a bubble of protection keeping the dark water at bay. He spotted a fish occasionally, lit by the light that attracted them. The spongy floor felt good on his feet. There were partitions and doors that led to other parts of the platform. Strange things were everywhere, instruments and vehicles that were definitely not of Earth origin. "Where is this place?"

"It is one of our undersea bases. We keep a few things here in case they are needed, but it is a refuge as much as a storage facility. In your terms, it could be called a Safe House."

"Why haven't we found this place?" asked Barclay. "It's well lit, and the pressure maintained."

"It is shielded," said the humanoid. "And we don't wish to be found."

"Is it air that I'm breathing?"

"We have duplicated the process that gills use to extract air from the sea. It happens automatically as the ocean currents press upon our dome."

"Do you need air to breathe?" asked Barclay.

"No, not necessarily," said the humanoid. "But you do."

"These lights," said Barclay. "Do you use electricity?"

"The lights are a trick of bio-luminescence."

"I see. This place is fascinating to me."

"I know," said the humanoid. "We are equally fascinated by your world."

"Do you mind if I look around?"

"Amanhatayotep brought you here, and so you are welcome."

"Huh?" said Barclay. "You mean Neptune?"

The humanoid laughed. "He likes the nickname you have given him, knowing you would have trouble pronouncing his real name. He tells me you have been a noble specimen for his research."

"His research!" said Barclay. "I thought it was *my* research."

"Maybe it is, but Amanhatayotep has been conducting his research much longer than you. He's very old."

"What research is that?" asked Barclay.

"Inter-species communication," said the humanoid. "He never told you?"

"No."

"He's like that," said the humanoid. "Plays the part of scientist quite well. He tries hard not to insert himself into the experiment."

"What do you mean?"

"He worked in one of your marine theme parks doing tricks, at least that's what the humans thought. It was his initial research, observing, learning your ways, looking for the people who would understand him and be willing to communicate. Then he had a breakthrough. He was transferred to a hands on exhibit in the park, part of a one-on-one dolphin experience."

"I've seen them," said Barclay. "They're very popular."

"Intimate contact with humans made a big difference," said the humanoid. "Dolphin and human opened their hearts to each other and in exchange he gave them rides, entertained them, and taught them things they'll never forget."

"He told you all this?"

"I've spent more time with him than you have," said the humanoid. "As I said, he's very old. We have been friends much longer than you have."

"Who are you?"

"Don't you know?" said the humanoid. "We are your ancestors, known by many names, Pleiadians, Extraterrestrials, the Gardeners of the Earth, and most commonly, aliens."

"Gardeners of the Earth?"

"We have planted many species throughout the galaxy," said the humanoid. "You are the Spirits of Freedom and Light."

"Tell that to the rest of humanity," he said. "Freedom is disappearing and Light is fading."

"This species will mature one day," said the humanoid. "We have high hopes."

"What, otherwise you clear the garden and plow us under for the next crop?"

Nonchalantly he replied, "Something like that."

"How long do I have to stay here?"

"You are free to go any time, but you should wait until the storm passes. We offer you temporary shelter," he said. "Amanhatayotep, I mean Neptune, told me he will come back for you when the danger has passed. Meanwhile, you are welcome here. Make yourself comfortable."

"Thank you," he said. He took a deep breath, clearing his mind. He easily achieved a mindful, meditative state, taking in every bit of his surroundings. This was something he wanted to remember. There were no light bulbs that he could see. The dome itself seemed to be the source of illumination. He shifted his weight feeling the soft response of the floor. It supported him and yet yielded, making it easy to move around. His bones and muscles felt relaxed and strong, almost as if the floor were healing him. Every step seemed to make him feel better. "Nice place you have here. Pressurized and safe. Great place to weather the storm."

"Amanhatayotep said you'd like it," said the humanoid. "He made all the arrangements for you to be here. Feel free to look around. For your own safety don't touch any controls. Now, if you'll excuse me, it is difficult for me to maintain a three dimensional presence. The floor helps with that but it can only do so much. We are higher dimensional beings, like you."

"Like me?"

"Yes," said the humanoid. "You have many bodies, all linked together. Some of them exist in higher realms, moving about conducting their own soul work. You are not aware of it because you are so focused on this reality. That makes it hard for you to imagine that there are other worlds in and around you."

"What do you mean?" asked Barclay.

"Let me put it another way," said the humanoid. "Just as I have difficulty maintaining a presence in your dimension, you would have trouble doing so in my dimension."

Barclay nodded.

"So you see, the differences between you and I are inconsequential, except I am not locked into a physical form for a finite lifetime. It is necessary for you, the only way to experience a reality this dense. Upon death you will absorb this form and your physical experience will transition into your higher self. Perhaps we will meet and talk when you are there."

"I'd like that," said Barclay.

"I will ascend now," said the humanoid. "The gray ones will help you with anything you need. Enjoy your stay."

The humanoid faded out, disappearing like an echo.

Barclay turned to the gray being. "Well then, buddy, I guess it's just you and me."

The gray being smiled and lovingly stared back at him through big, black eyes.

# Chapter 12

## Keep Your Eye on the Storm

"As you can see by the map I have displayed, there is now a class five hurricane moving in place right over the target coordinates you provided," said Simian. He smiled, then reached for the tray of money only to have his arm grabbed by Gort.

"Let him hold it Gort," said Rothschild. "But only that. You have not earned it yet Mr. Jacks. The demonstration is not over. We must see what happens next. A hundred and seventy mile an hour winds, you say? How long will they last? What about the inland path? How far will it go?" He took a sip of the drink in front of him. "No. The demonstration will be over when I say it is over and you will be paid when it is over. Are we clear?"

"Yes, sir," said Simian. He stared into the monitor watching the swirling bands change as the radar updated them. The aerial imagery showed some kind of structures on the ground. *It was a clear day there this morning for them. I wonder how they are faring now?*

His thoughts began to wander. He looked over at Rothschild. The fat man motioned to Gort for something. Simian continued to be lost in his silent, inner debate.

*Why these coordinates,* thought Simian. *Surely our government will hear about this, the sudden appearance of a hurricane. Hopefully they'll never be able to trace it to me. They'll blame it on global warming, climate change, or a bad year for El Niño, something like that.*

*That might be their public statement. The government is good about denying any culpability. But they know about the weather control project. They can figure it out. Get the FBI and the CIA on it. They could trace it to me. I will be called to task for my crimes.*

He started thinking of Tinker. How many lives affected? At least one already. He studied the imagery again. There seemed to be more trees than structures, but it still looked inhabited. He turned and stared at the money, trying to guess the population and divide the number of lost lives into the amount of money. What would it come out to be? Probably somewhere between one hundred dollars to a thousand dollars a life. Maybe the old saying is true. Life is cheap.

The anxiety on his face did not escape Rothschild. "Gort. Fix Mr. Jacks another drink. I'll take one as well."

"That's okay, Mr. Rothschild," he said. "I don't need one."

"Nonsense! Gort, make it happen."

Drinks were served. Simian stared through the bottom of the glass at the distorted world it created. He downed the drink in a gulp and set the glass on the table. Winds were hitting a hundred and seventy five now and rising. It was officially a category five. He could only imagine the damage and destruction. In addition to the radar, he had a news feed window open on the computer. It flashed a story about Mexico put on high alert. The population was being evacuated and sheltered in advance of the storm. Rothschild reached over and shut the news feed down.

Simian's mind eased. Better odds, he thought. With more people in shelters and less casualties, the price of human life might rise.

A strange feeling came over him. Trading money for lives, was it not an evil akin to slavery? Again he thought of Tinker. *Poor Tinker, mauled by a bear. I should have driven him to the gate.*

"Are you okay, Mr. Jacks?" asked Rothschild. "You are welcome to go to your room and rest."

"No," he said.

"How about another drink, then," he said. "For someone who didn't want one, you finished yours rather quickly."

"No," said Simian. "I don't need to rest. I'll stay here and sit this out. I want to see what's going to happen."

"What do you expect to happen?" asked Rothschild.

"The eye of the storm is deceptively calm. People can be lulled by a sense of false safety, wandering out of their shelters. The calm will be short lived as the hurricane continues on its track and the winds pelt the area with devastating force from the opposite direction."

"I see," said Rothschild.

Simian could swear the fat man was salivating like he was hearing the menu choices from a waiter at a fine restaurant. He continued his report. "There will also be severe coastal flooding. The eye of the storm may be calm, but it is a low pressure area surrounded by a wall of wind and water. It has the effect of a soda straw, sucking water up into it, raising the tide as much as five to ten feet."

"Lovely," said Rothschild. "Anything else?"

"Insects sometimes get trapped in the eye. They carry diseases such as dengue fever, West Nile Virus, and other things. Often there is an outbreak of health problems after the storm passes."

"You don't say," said Rothschild. He downed his drink and licked his lips, a grin of satisfaction erupting over his chin. Gort placed a fresh one in front of him and took the old one away.

"Let's see the final result of the demonstration. If any of those things happen, I will call it a success."

Simian watched the fat man raise the glass to his mouth and take another sip. He was immersed in pleasure, but it was not from the alcohol. This went deeper. *Is there no conscience in this man?* he thought.

Rothschild stared at the screen. "Yes, let's see what happens next."

A creepy feeling descended over Simian. Again he thought of Tinker. He quickly tried to let it pass but the feeling refused to go away. He heard Tinker's voice inside his head, an imaginary friend that said to him, "You made your moral choice. Let's see what happens next."

What else could happen? Simian began to ponder Tinker's fate. What if his death was not a coincidence? He looked at the money, thinking about the cost of human life, thinking about his own life. There was a lot of money on that tray. Would he live long enough to spend it?

"Yes," he said, deep in thought as he echoed Rothschild's words. "Let's see what happens next."

# Chapter 13

## The Visitors

Randall awoke, unaware of how much time had passed. He felt restless. He stood up and stretched. There was an ache in his thigh, a pain he could not fathom. His skin itched and even his morning Kriya and yoga practice did not help. He grunted with the effort, feeling like the old man he was. Age had been kind to him, and he was well past what everyone called retirement age. He stopped counting the years after he stopped celebrating his birthday. There were more important things to celebrate after all.  He was voraciously hungry, ready to consume anything and everything. It was not often he felt like this.

"Ah, you're up," said the doctor entering the room. "And you've been moving and exercising I see. Excellent."

"What is this pain in my thigh?" asked Randall.

"You've been in a deep, therapeutic sleep," said the doctor. "It often affects memory. You might not recall our conversation, but you damaged your femur." The doctor went to the wall monitor, logged in and checked some figures. "You're just about healed. The skin itch should go away shortly. The pain will become a dull ache and within a week or so it will be gone."

"I damaged my femur?" asked Randall. The Kriya had cleared his mind but not his memory. He took another deep breath, connecting with the unseen part of himself where all memory dwells. He suddenly saw the past with clarity. "Yes. I damaged my femur. As in broke it, correct?"

The doctor narrowed his eyes. "Yes, perhaps you do remember our earlier conversation."

"How did it heal so quickly?" asked Randall. "No, wait!" He thought for a moment. "You used what you called accelerated field growth, am I right?"

"Yes," said the doctor. "Remarkable. It's rare anyone is able to recall details of their early treatment, especially with the time modulation caused by the field generator."

"You don't say," said Randall, trying to process what the doctor just said. "I still have questions."

"I imagine so," said the doctor.

Randall closed his eyes and concentrated, his memory beginning to provide details as he focused. "You called this place Tobit," he said.

"Yes," said the doctor.

"But you never said where Tobit is. Are we in Mexico?"

"More like under Mexico I might say."

Randall moved towards the window. The doctor joined him, pressing something on the side of the window pane. The shade lifted and Randall got his first view of Tobit.

In a glance Randall knew he was somewhere beyond imagination.

"Am I dead?" he asked.

"No," said the doctor. "You're in Tobit."

"Where is this place?" asked Randall.

"I can't give you exact figures, but we are deep beneath the crust of your Earth." said the doctor.

Randall turned to face him. "It's your Earth, too, you know," he said.

"Of course," said the doctor. "Do you feel up to some company? You have visitors."

"What?" said Randall. "Oh, sure."

The doctor stepped outside for a moment, returning with a man and two women. Randall didn't recognize them, he had hoped it was Ravi or someone from the Eighth Day Village of the Sun, here to take him home. At the very least he expected the people who had pulled him from the water and brought him to the hospital. But it was neither.

"Randall, these people represent the Department of Immigration, Department of Justice, and the Department of Readjustment," said the doctor. "They would like to talk to you." He bowed to the group saying, "I'll leave introductions to you then." He left them alone in the room.

"Mr. Randall, my name is Keeting," said a well dressed woman. "I'm with the Department of Immigration. I'd like to welcome you to Tobit."

"And I'm Penny," said the other woman, a bit older but immaculate still. "I'm here to help you readjust."

"And I'm Biggs," said the man. "Department of Justice. I'm here to make sure everything proceeds according to our laws."

"I'm overwhelmed," said Randall. "You're all here for me?"

"That's right," said Keeting, smiling. "I'm here to swear you in as a probationary citizen, along with all the rights associated."

"What rights would they be?" asked Randall.

"First of all, free medical treatment, just as you have received here," she said.

"That's useful," he said.

"Would you care to take the oath now?" she asked.

"In a moment," he said. "I'd like to ask a few more questions if I may."

"Of course," she said.

He turned to the older woman. "For one thing, Penny, what do I need to adjust to?"

"Well, for one thing, your new life here," she said. "I was able to secure an apartment for you close to where you were found, in the beautiful park district of Tobit. Many of your kind live there."

"My kind?" he asked.

"We're only trying to help you fit in," she said. "We've found that many immigrants need the support and bonding they can only find between their own people."

"I see," said Randall. "My own people. What about work? Will you find my dharma for me as well?"

"That's just what I mean," she said. "A member of your own group might know what dharma means, and if it means work, well, I've arranged for you to have six to ten months to find your niche. And I'll be here to help you."

"That's wonderful," said Randall, a little too sarcastically.

"Don't be that way, Randall," said Biggs. "These women are trying to help you."

"In case you don't know it, I already have work, and a community of my own people." He emphasized his words to Penny and Keeting.

"Do you really expect to be able to find your way back to the surface?" asked Biggs.

"I found my way down here, didn't I?" asked Randall.

"By accident," said Keeting. "Like all those surface dwellers that happen to find their way here."

"And do you keep all of them here as prisoners?" asked Randall.

"They are not prisoners," said Penny. "We integrate them into our society, help them adjust to their situation."

Randall looked at Biggs. "Is it against the law for them to leave this place?"

"Not exactly," he said.

"Don't worry, Mr. Randall," said Penny. "We're are here to help you."

"Okay then," he said. "I need help getting back to my community, the Eighth Day Village of the Sun."

"I don't know if we can do that," said Biggs. "Besides, the law requires that you remain here."

"In this hospital?" demanded Randall.

"No, in Tobit," he said.

"No, no, no," said Randall. "That can't happen."

"It must," said Biggs. "Every surface dweller who finds their way down here is given the opportunity to join our community."

"Surface dweller?" asked Randall. "You have me pigeonholed."

Biggs looked perplexed. Penny turned towards him and said, "Colorful language these crusters have. I've heard that one before. It means we've given him no options. No alternative."

"That's right," said Randall.

Biggs stepped forward, turning Randall to look out the window. "Do you realize what an opportunity this is, Mr. Randall. Why don't you give it a chance? We have no wars here. We have found the cures for what ails us, both in body and in mind. There is no greed here, and so there is abundance for everyone. You will be free here to pursue your dreams, Mr. Randall."

Randall stared out the window. He watched a monorail train approach, noticing finally that it was floating and unattached to anything. In the background was the most beautiful city he had ever seen, except in his dreams and visions of the celestial realms. Bright buildings of every shape and form were everywhere. Tall spires reached up towards the sky. It was then he saw that there were no shadows, that the light that illuminated this place was something other than the sun, something with no distinct source.

"What if my dream was to return to my world?" asked Randall.

"Accept it," said Biggs. "You're an insider now. Spend some time here and you'll see how much better life can be."

"Insider?"

"As inside the Earth," said Biggs. "Tobit is one of several cities that exist inside the hollow Earth."

"We really want nothing to do with surface dwellers," said Penny. "But when you people do find your way down here, we try to accommodate you."

"But we must maintain our secrecy," said Biggs. "Your world must never know of our existence."

"And why is that?" asked Randall.

"We want nothing to do with what goes on up there," said Keeting. "Can you imagine what our world would be like if we adopted the ways of your society?"

"No," said Randall. "I can't imagine. I have no basis to judge. I know absolutely nothing about your world."

"I would be glad to take you on a tour," said Penny. "Just as soon as you take the oath of citizenship."

"I need to take an oath of citizenship for a tour?" asked Randall. "I don't suppose you've ever heard of tourism. Very popular in Mexico."

Keeting looked perplexed.

"It's the name they have given to a large expanse of land on the surface," explained Penny. "They are extremely territorial up there."

"I know that Penny," said Biggs.

"I didn't," said Keeting.

Biggs focused on Randall. "You will have many benefits as member of our society," he said. "Our ways take a higher path than those on the surface. We focus on peace and harmony here."

"It's a better place to live," said Keeting. "You'll see."

"Can I take the tour before I decide?" asked Randall.

"I'm afraid we can't do that," said Penny.

"You see the need for us to remain hidden," said Biggs. "Your world would infect us with your ways. Our pure State would be lost."

"I see that," said Randall. "But surely there are exceptions? Trusted friends who are allowed to return."

"I'm afraid there are no exceptions," said Biggs. "You must remain here. We have been dealing with this situation for centuries. It is our way. It is our law."

"But what if I promise to keep your secret?" he said.

"We have tried that in the past," said Biggs. "Usually when they return, the surface dweller tries to profit somehow from their experience and the time they spent down here. Our technology is superior to yours, especially when it is applied to health and spirituality. Naturally we have to take precautions. Many of the tunnels that lead here from the surface have traps and uncomfortable vibrations. Only fools tempt fate. Very few find their way here, but when they do..."

Keeting interrupted him. "We try to accommodate them."

"Your coming here was an accident," said Biggs.

"Yes," said Penny. "You did not seek us out intentionally."

Randall smiled seeing the kindness in their eyes. "I'm overwhelmed."

"Maybe you're ready to take the oath of citizenship now," asked Keeting.

"The doctor has released you," said Penny. "Once you're finished with the oath I'll take you to your apartment and show you the benefits of living here."

"It's your best option," said Biggs.

"No, it's not," said Randall. "I'd like to appeal to a higher authority."

There was silence as Keeting and Penny both looked towards Biggs.

"How did you know about our appeal process?" asked Biggs. "You're not a spy, are you?"

"No," said Randall. "Every civilized group of people has an appeal process. I want an appeal. Take me to a higher authority."

"On what grounds?"

"On the grounds that you are stealing my life," said Randall. "I am a leader in my spiritual community on the surface. My work lies there, not in Tobit."

"But you haven't given us a chance," said Biggs. "Do you know what you are passing up?"

"Are you certain you want to leave?" asked Penny. "You could easily find a new spiritual purpose here. It's very peaceful. We have been compared to the Heavenly Fields, excellent for meditation and contemplation."

Randall breathed a sigh. "Look, I've heard of you. We have legends up above about the hollow earth, stories and superstitions. Most are fiction. You are not what I expected."

Keeting smiled.

"What are you hiding from anyway?" asked Randall. The world upstairs is in turmoil. It's obvious from your appearance that we share a common ancestry. Why not help your fellow man?"

"Spiritual leaders have tried to help you surface dwellers," he said. "Many at the cost of their life. You people are cruel. Countless times throughout history you have tortured and killed anyone who does not follow your way of thinking."

"And without help or change, that will continue," said Randall. "I work for peace, just like you. I can judge my fellow man, make myself feel superior, or even hide my head in the sand like you do, but I prefer to work for change. True, my world is not perfect. I find it horribly flawed at times, but I am not about to abandon it."

Biggs eyed him up. "If that's the way you feel."

"It's the way it is," said Randall.

Biggs shook his head as he turned to the others. "Come on. I'll contact the tribunal and make the arrangements. Ladies, your work here is done."

Keating looked at Randall. "Does this mean you won't be taking the oath?"

# Chapter 14

## Act or React?

"A category five hurricane?" said President Carson Whiteweather. He looked out the window of the oval office at the clear skies above Washington. It was humid outside. The city was built on a swamp and despite the buildings, pavement, and other man made changes the climate remained the same as any swamp: hot and humid. He thought about the Eighth Day Village of the Sun and wondered what the skies above them might look like. "What makes you think it was man made?"

"It's not quite hurricane season, for one," said Juliana.

"Climate change has caused many problems," he said. "Could this be one of them?"

"You know our climate. We had clear skies this morning with a forecast for more of the same. This storm was sudden. I spoke with Gaia and she knows this is not natural. She is in pain. Then there is the odd coincidence that it is headed directly for the Eighth Day Village of the Sun. The strongest storm imaginable, Carson!"

Whiteweather turned to his security team, covering the mouthpiece of his phone. "Give me a moment of privacy," he said, knowing that he never actually had such a moment, that all his conversations and movements were recorded. It didn't bother him. History would show that all those in power were still human. The secret service team respectfully left the room.

"When are you coming home?" he asked.

She slouched down in the gallery seat and lowered her voice. "When this is over," she said. "I miss you so much."

"You're the First Lady. You should be here with me."

"It's just as hard for me to live with our arrangement," she said. "You have no idea, Carson. The yearnings you have stirred in me..."

He drew a sigh, thinking of the Tantric moments they had embraced together. He was an Army General before he was elected President, used to command and getting what he wanted. Like most men, this extended into his relationships, but he found that the normal rules did not apply when it came to the High Priestess of the Eighth Day Village of the Sun. If he wanted a relationship with this woman, it would be on her terms. He could not argue or debate those terms. They both knew that she would never belong to him entirely, that she belonged to the Village, to Gaia, to the world and her dharma. It made her an excellent First Lady and when he married her it was on these conditions.

Likewise she knew that this was the answer for her, a powerful soulmate that shared her vision. Their combined abilities could shake the world and change it for the better. Despite the physical distance between them they faced their problems together, their time apart just as precious as the time they spent together. Phone calls between them like this came as often as needed.

"I want you," she said, her breath deep and raspy.

He squirmed, the leather chair squeaking beneath him. "To answer your question, yes, we do have weather control," he said. "There is a base in Nevada, very experimental."

"I knew it," she said.

"Okay, but who would do such a thing?"

"I have my suspicions," she said.

"I do too," he said, careful not to mention any names. There is no privacy for the President. "Proving it would not be easy. We are not the only country that has been developing weather control tools."

"I know that," she said.

"How bad is it?" he asked.

"I told you. Category five. Wind is over one hundred and seventy

88

miles per hour at the last report."

"I'm prepared to extend international aide," he said. "I'll send the military and FEMA."

She laughed. "For a vacation maybe," she said. "You know full well that we can take care of ourselves. The architects of the Eighth Day Village planned on two hundred and twenty miles per hour winds. The structures near the water have breakaway walls and other safeguards. Our shelters were modeled after bomb shelters, the entrances positioned out of the wind at the end of long concrete corridors. Even our communications are shielded, otherwise I think the towers would be down and I wouldn't be talking to you now."

"Okay, okay," said Carson. "I just want you to know I'm here for you."

"Don't worry about us," she said. "We have the labor and the resources to rebuild if necessary. You answered my question. Now get back to taking care of the country you love." She blew a breath of air. "God I miss you. You obstinate, difficult, caring, loving man."

He chuckled. "Okay. I have to go. Got an important meeting in a few minutes."

She looked down at the table watching a group assemble. Darius motioned to her up in the gallery. "Evidently so do I," she said.

"I love you. Call me later. Let me know you're safe."

"I'm in the emergency operations center here," she said. "As safe as it gets."

She did not let him hang up, instead she taunted him for a minute, saying things that would only make him want her more.

A secret service man in a nearby hidden room stopped the recording tapes, his face red with embarrassment.

Yes, history will prove that the Kings, Presidents, even the Generals; all the people in power were and still are human.

She hung up the phone and headed back towards her seat. A

meeting was about to start. Slots around the table filled up as representatives from the emergency support functions crowded around. Darius urged the stragglers to hurry up.

"We are approaching zero hour, people," said Darius. "Gather up. It's time to make decisions."

Faces around the table were grim.

Tamara, a representative of the Human Services group, spoke first. "What's wrong with waiting it out like we normally do?"

"We're going to do that anyway," said Darius. "We can't waste this opportunity. This is a chance to pit our intellect and resources against a hurricane."

Juliana joined in as she sat down. "Gaia has asked for our help. How can we refuse?"

"Yes," said Manny. "She asked us to restore balance. What exactly does that mean?"

"She also said the storm is unstoppable," said Caroline.

"She meant that she could not stop it," said Juliana. "At least not alone. All Gaia can do is wait it out. But this is painful to her, unnatural. The longer this goes on, the more she suffers."

"So we must do what we can, or at least try," said Darius.

"I agree," said Manny. "We hide from storms all the time. Let's try something different."

"Okay," said Stine. "But what? We've been discussing lots of ideas."

"We are less than thirty minutes from the eye of the storm." said Caroline. "That doesn't give us very much time. It we are going to try something I suggest we act quickly."

"What's the plan, then?" asked Darius. "I'm open to ideas." He turned towards Caroline. "You mentioned low pressure. Have you made your calculations? Do we have a way to hold the storm in place?"

"I'm not sure it's possible," said Caroline. "Pressure inside the eye measures eight hundred and ninety two millibars now, way lower than I expected."

"What does that mean?" asked Darius.

"The normal, average atmospheric pressure at sea level is over a thousand millibars," said Caroline. "We would have to counteract the low pressure and raise it up that high. I don't see a way to do that."

"We have powerful fans and turbines," said Stine. "Could that help?"

"I don't know if it will be enough," she said. "Fans and turbines would just push air around. We're talking about an order of magnitude."

"We were thinking of using the cooling tunnels," said Darius. "They go through the mountain and open up on the other side. It's a trick to make our climate a little more comfortable than it normally would be."

"Cooling tunnels?" asked Caroline,

"We have air conditioning but it is more practical and cheaper to let the Earth do the job," said Darius. "They're closed off and secured for the emergency, but we can easily open them up."

"We've been looking at pressure," said Manny. "How about temperature? Hurricanes need warm water to survive. We discussed somehow using refrigeration to calm it down."

"Nice idea," said Caroline.

"What if we try both at the same time?" he asked.

"It's a question of power," said Caroline. "A hurricane can contain over five hundred trillion watts of energy. Do you have enough to counteract that?"

"That's lot more power than we can generate," said Darius. "More than the world generates in electricity."

"Much more," said Stine.

"Maybe we can take a lesson from martial arts," said Manny. "Judo uses the opponent's strength against themselves."

"Nice analogy, Manny," said Stine. "Why not hit Goliath with a slingshot while we're at it."

"You're forgetting," said Juliana. "Gaia is willing to help. She has resources, planetary energy, that we don't have. If we all work together with her, it might be possible."

Darius checked some figures. "Village power is high. We could crank up the torus and boost it to maximum."

"The molecular springs are charged to capacity," said Stine. "Rain keeps them fed with potential energy. And the hurricane is producing a lot of rain."

"I like that idea," said Caroline. "Use the power of the storm to defeat it. There's your judo, Manny."

Manny was toying with his bottle again. "What we are up against is far more powerful than us. I say we throw everything we got at it at once. If it has the strength you say, then we're going to need it all: temperature, pressure, power, Gaia."

"Even with all that, counteracting temperature and pressure may not be enough to do it," said Caroline. "It would help if we had something more."

"We can try the LRAD while we're in the eye," said Darius. "Low range acoustics may help slice through the rain bands. It would be small but disruptive. Caroline, what would be the effect of punching a hole in the eye wall?"

"It would cause a leak from high pressure to low. The problem is the hole would be whisked away by the wind the moment it was created."

"We don't know that," said Manny. "Everything we try today is experimental."

"Well, by David, there's my slingshot," said Stine. He got up from the table. "I think we can configure the array to widen the acoustic field.

I'll go check with operations. We'll at least be ready to try it."

"Will LRAD interfere with anything else we're trying to do?" asked Manny.

"No, I don't think so," said Caroline. "It's a good idea, though. I can't help but think we're spitting into the wind. Our attempts to raise the temperature may be as feeble as putting a glass full of ice on a kitchen counter and expecting it to cool the whole house down."

"We have very efficient and powerful refrigeration," said Darius. "And I have a bigger plan in mind."

"Okay, so it's like putting a cooler of ice on the counter instead of a glass?" said Caroline.

The representative from the Human Services group spoke up. "How about prayer? Can we try that?"

"Prayer works," said Juliana. "Especially when it's done right. Selfless prayer for the safety of others. Good idea, Tamara. I'll contact the meditation groups in the other shelters." She picked up a communication handset.

"How does that work?" asked Caroline.

"Prayer is willful," said Tamara. "It can change things. Have you ever tried to dissipate a cloud using the force of your mind?" asked Juliana.

"What?" asked Caroline.

"Laying down, looking up at the sky. Have you ever tried to focus your will and open a hole in the clouds?"

"Can's say that I have," said Caroline.

"Try it next time," said Juliana. "It works. Prayer is like that, only more powerful."

"What about my idea?" asked Manny. "What if we capped the top of the storm with a force field?"

"Capped it?" asked Darius. "What do you mean?"

93

Manny spun the bottle creating a vortex. "Ever do this in the bathtub or sink?"

"When I was a little girl, maybe," said Caroline.

"It may be possible to deploy a force field while we are in the eye of the storm," said Manny. "It will be calm."

"Do you know how high you would have to go to cap it?" asked Caroline. "Probably fifty thousand feet, maybe more."

"You're both on the wrong track," said Darius. "Force field technology will not work."

"No?" said Manny. "What then?"

"Anti gravity," said Darius.

"What are you going to do?" asked Juliana. "Lift the hurricane up into space?"

"Is that even possible?" asked Caroline.

"Here's my thinking," said Darius. "A force field would require a lot of energy. Anti-gravity uses anti-gravitons which take less energy to create and direct."

"I see what you might be getting at," said Manny. "I can easily integrate your idea into my plan, Darius."

"I still don't get it," said Caroline.

"You don't have to," said Darius.

"You don't have time," said Caroline. "The eye wall is less than ten miles away. You've got maybe a half hour, forty five minutes."

Darius nodded towards Manny, who got up and left the table.

He walked off just as Stine returned. "The technical team will be ready to deploy the LRAD against the storm," said Stine. "They think it's a great idea. They're going to do some slight modifications to focus the beam better, try tryto make it work more like a jaackhammer. They think it will be easier to aim it and poke holes in the eye wall."

94

"That's encouraging," said Caroline. "But small holes may not have the desired effect. High speed winds create low pressure as they pass over a tube. The venturi effect."

"They thought of that," said Stine. "They are also creating a few other programs to try. One of them is a shotgun blast that would open multiple holes at once."

"Great," said Darius. "So we have the LRAD, force fields, refrigeration, anti gravity, and pressure."

"And prayer," said Tamara. "Don't forget prayer."

"That's everything we have to throw at it," said Caroline. "But it still may not be enough."

"Let's remain optimistic," said Tamara.

"It's going to take all of us working together to do this," said Darius. "Stine, you have the LRAD. Caroline will continue to monitor the storm and keep us all updated. Juliana will let Gaia know what we are doing. I can assemble the experts to handle temperature and pressure."

"That leaves Manny with his giant hand," said Stine. "This should be interesting."

Manny came over from information and planning accompanied by a young lady. "This is Cara, my deputy chief. She will be at the table with you in my absence. I'll have my comm on and will report my progress."

Stine stood up. "I'll be with the technical branch ready with the LRAD." He was off.

Caroline was encouraged until she saw the hurricane data. "Oh, no. The eye has shrunk. The storm is intensifying. Sustained winds have jumped to a hundred and eighty five miles per hour now. We definitely have a pinhole eye."

"Did I hear you say a pinhole eye?" asked Manny.

"Yes," said Caroline. "They are the worst, found at the center of some of the most deadly hurricanes in recorded history. It's picked up speed, moving towards us quickly. You may not have enough time for your plan."

"How small is this pinhole?" he asked.

"Less than five miles wide and shrinking," she said.

"What a stroke of luck," said Manny. He ran off excitedly.

Darius stared into the wall monitors. Trees were down, pathways clogged with debris, the beach was being pounded by ten foot surf. One of the sailboats in the marina had broken loose. It was laying sideways on the beach, rocking with the force of the wind. Manny's beachside hut was taking a beating. One image just shook, the camera on the pole it was mounted on swaying in the wind.

"Whatever we're going to do, Darius, we better do it quickly."

"Can you think of anything else we might need?" he asked.

"Prayer," said Juliana. "Lots of prayer."

# Chapter 15

## Confronting the Self Who Is Not the Self

Singh crawled through mud and dirt in the low, narrow corridor, a passage no higher than five feet. He felt insects dropping from above, creeping across his skin in the semi darkness. The flashlight swept across the floor and walls revealing snakes, lizards, and jungle vermin also seeking shelter. He projected a shield of protection around himself using the energy of his lightbody. The snakes slithered away, avoiding him completely, the insects didn't seem to be affected. He imagined even greater threats and he fought his emotions in a battle with intellect. Instead of panicking, he turned his attention to the walls. Beneath the bugs and debris were hieroglyphics and paintings, a message from the past.

He understood the writing. One message warned him of a trap up ahead. He carefully inched his way forward, following instructions as he read them. The corridor turned a few times, went up and down, both at angles and vertically. It even branched once, and it was clear that the designers of this passageway wanted to disorient and confuse anyone who came here.

The final stretch of corridor sloped upward where it opened into a large room. The temple was small judging from the outside. Most of the inner space was within this room. Singh stood up releasing his anxiety and claustrophobia. He moved the flashlight around, studying his surroundings.

There was a flat stone table at one end, an alter. Clay bowls, urns, and jars rested on it among the dust and dirt. He looked inside one, the crumbled remains of something long ago turned to powder. He inhaled deeply, the slight medicinal smell of plants making him wonder what they were. Dipping his finger into the mixture, he raised it to his lips and gave it a slight taste. *Ritualistic herbs used in some ceremony,* he thought. *It could be anything. Ayahuasca,*

*mushrooms, or even toad milk, things used by the shaman to*
*communicate with the spirits of the jungle and the world beyond.*

He spit the powder out, wondering what the purpose of the temple could be. He saw writing on the walls but they gave him no clue. It all read like gibberish from a children's book. The few pictures showed people planting crops, preparing food, running, playing games, and building structures, things he already knew through his study of history.

There was a raised receptacle in the center of the alter. He was drawn to it. There was a battery powered lantern in his backpack. He took it out, turned it on and set it on the alter. The room burst with light adding warmth to the dark, carved stone walls. There was another level of writing above the pictures on the walls, a border close to the ceiling. He studied the writing, still looking for clues about the purpose of this temple. This was not gibberish, instead readable text that he devoured like a hungry traveler. He breathed a sigh of relief realizing the temple was not a place used for death and human sacrifice. Instead, this was a place for the training of shaman and medicine men, people dedicated to the healing arts. From the writing he learned that the priests could somehow cure both physical and spiritual ailments using the objects in the room.

He looked again in the raised receptacle. It was an essential part of the ritual. He dug into it, clearing away centuries of dirt that had settled inside. His efforts revealed a finely polished jewel a little larger than a softball. He rubbed it clean with a spare shirt from his backpack, the smooth surface beginning to glow under the lantern light.

"Is this what I'm supposed to retrieve?" he said out loud. He expected Ixpetz to answer him, but it remained still and quiet within the stone walls. He gripped the jewel with both hands attempting to remove it from the receptacle. It was heavy and he strained under the weight, unable to move it so much as a micron.

"I guess not," he said. He went back to studying the writing on the walls, his only clue to solving this mystery. "It might be time for enlightenment." he said, finding a comfortable spot to sit.

There was one set of tools that had always benefited his study of something new and strange. Contemplation and meditation. He closed his eyes as he focused his intentions. Several deep breaths later he entered a trance.

He achieved a deep state quickly, the result of years of practice. He thought about projecting his astral form to check in with the Village. Before he could concentrate his efforts he heard noises around him. There was a low growl, fierce and ferocious. He opened his eyes to see a jaguar in the room with him, staring at him like he was tonight's feast. It made another growl.

"How did you get in here?" he asked nervously. Like the snakes, he tried to project a psychic shield around him, a band of protection and white light. Unlike the snakes, the jaguar remained still, staring at him like he was waiting for the dinner bell to chime.

"I guess I forgot to shut the front door," he said.

The jaguar let out another low growl.

# Chapter 16

# The Appeal

Randall was taken to a high court much like the ones he had seen on the surface. They all had a common theme, a large building with oversized rooms making the humans seem small and insignificant. There was always a raised bench where the higher authority sat in judgment. You had to look up at them, another trick to make you seem small. Three ornately dressed characters sat there now staring down at him, a man and two women with serious faces and demeanor. They even had the legal lingo of the high courts. The one in the center spoke. "The Tobit Appeals Committee will now come to order. The tribunal has been seated. I am Astra. My fellow adjudicators are Reena and Wezley. Come forward, Randall from the surface world, and state your case."

Randall stood and composed himself with dignity, clearing his throat before beginning. "Your hospitality is gracious and your offers tempting, but I wish to return to my own community on the surface world. I am just that, a surface dweller, unfit for life down here. In the short time I have been exposed to your world, I see you have solved many of the problems that have plagued mankind. I applaud your technical abilities and your scientific achievements. Your medicine is far beyond anything I have seen above, as is your level of spiritual development."

He took a deep breath. "I would like to address that if I may. I sense a prejudice against surface dwellers. I myself am inclined to agree with your assessment of the species, however I endeavor to be less judgmental of my fellow man. One of our greatest spiritual leaders once said, "Judge not, lest ye be judged." It means, don't jump to conclusions until you know all the facts. The only judgment we face is from our God and ourselves. Most of us have a conscience and know when we have erred. To help with that, our spiritual leaders have taught us compassion and forgiveness.

"The other issue I want to bring up is trust. Just because some of 'my kind' showed less than perfect behavior in the past, it doesn't mean that we all are the same. We face each other as individuals. Humans come in all varieties of shapes and kinds. With everything going on up there, we surface dwellers are put to the test daily. We have to make decisions that affect our linear lives. I ask you to trust me. I have more important work to do than trying to profit from this encounter. I've been offered better, and I have not compromised my principles. You must see that."

Wezley held up his hand. "You are right, Randall," he said. "We don't see that." He turned towards the tribunal. "We know nothing about this man. Perhaps we should put him in the chamber of truth and see for ourselves what lies hidden in his soul."

"It would certainly save time," said Reena. "This one is pretty long winded, but then, most of these surface dwellers love to talk."

"Agreed," said Astra. She made a quick hand motion.

A man came up to Randall. He gripped his arm and escorted him to a square chamber near the wall, vertical and slightly bigger than a coffin. It had a clear door over the front. Randall entered at the man's urging.

Lights came on, a full spectrum of analysis. Randall felt calm, loved, open and vulnerable. Life could not have been any better. He smiled.

The review panel smiled as well. Through their technology they could see many aspects of the jewel known as Baba Randall. Every human has many facets, some reflecting darkness, some glistening like starlight. Randall stood peacefully while the tribunal processed what they were seeing.

Astra finally spoke. "This being speaks truthfully and can be trusted." She made another gesture and the man returned to the coffin and released Randall. Once again he stood before them looking up into faces he could not read.

"But we have our rules," said Wezley. "Our privacy cannot be violated."

"I don't know why you feel like that," said Randall. "We can do so much for each other."

"You mean we can do so much more for you."

"And the other surface dwellers," said Reena. "You may speak the truth, but given the chance you would exploit us and our technology."

"Exploit is such an ugly word," said Randall. "Believe me though, I've been in your position. I've been exploited and it doesn't feel good." He cleared is throat. "Let me tell you a story."

"Oh, no," said Reena. "More talk."

"What does this have to do with us?" asked Wezley. "Or your case for that matter."

"Hear me out," said Randall.

"The rules of the appeal say we must let him speak his peace," said Astra.

"Thank you," said Randall, again clearing his throat. "There was a war above."

"There are always wars above," said Reena.

"This one ended with a nation divided," said Randall. "So divided that a wall was built in the capital city that broke the citizens in two. It was symbolic, for the whole country was divided by the victors, a people once united, broken by a political battle of ideologies. Under the rule of two opposing conquerors, one side of the broken nation prospered while the other suffered. After many years, the war was forgotten and the victors tired of fighting over the broken nation. They finally released their grasp and left the citizens alone. What do you think they did?"

"Knowing your people, they turned on them and waged war against the oppressors."

Randall smiled. "No, they chose a path called reunification. The wall was the first thing to go. One side was poor, the other rich, yet they were still united by language and culture. They remembered their past when they were all one. Each then embraced their other half with open arms, all in the name of reunification."

"Again I ask, what has this to do with us or your case?" asked Wezley.

"Reunification," said Randall. "Consider the possibility that we surface dwellers share the same language and ancient history as you. The same dreams of governance and spirituality. The same hopes for our future. Would you not serve a higher purpose by helping those less fortunate? Teach us what you have learned. Show us by example how to find our way to a better life. Would not both our cultures improve if we moved forward together?"

"And what could we learn from you?" asked Astra.

"Compassion, love, what it is like to give," said Randall.

"We have all that," said Astra.

"We are aware of your world," said Reena. "We have experience with surface dwellers over time. They are discontent, as if paradise was not enough to satisfy their quest for the banal."

"So you have studied us a long time," said Randall. "Are you not clever enough to figure out a way to introduce us to a higher purpose?"

"Teachers have appeared on the surface," said Astra. "Look at the result. You even argue about the teachings."

"Your kind will eventually destroy itself," said Reena. "Unlike you, we are not interested in the conquest of the earth. It is more prudent for us to wait out our time."

There was silence. The tribunal looked down on Randall. He shook his head sadly. Wezley felt his dismay and tried to be encouraging. "Maybe one day we can emerge from hiding and seek the reunification you talk of," he said. "For now, your weapons and your way of life keep us down here. It's not safe for us on the surface."

"There is nothing more to say," said Astra. "We shall pause and deliberate. You will wait in the chamber of truth until we return."

Randall was once again escorted to the glass coffin and placed inside. The machine glowed, warm and loving, embracing him as a mother would embrace her child.

# Chapter 17

## Oceans Away

Franklin Van Dorn was near exhaustion. His arms and legs ached. He went between sculling on the surface to resting slightly below the waves. Despite the relatively calm water, he was still trapped in the eye, forced to constantly swim for survival. The walls were closing in on him. He could easily see the rain and wind swirling all around him. Through tricks of perspective, he always thought they were close, ready to pull and push him around at their violent whim.

His jaw ached from gripping the rebreather in his mouth. His lips were beginning to chafe. Salt water ran up his nostrils at times making him cough. He longed to stand on solid earth again. He wished he had grabbed a life preserver or jacket from the boat. Amazing what a difference a little bit of flotation makes.

His ears popped. Pressure was stretching his eardrums, an effect of the low pressure in the storm's eye. The saltwater sucked every bit of moisture from his skin, adding to his fatigue. He had no idea where he was or where the storm was headed. For all he knew he would never see land again. He worried about sharks, holding fast to a strategy, trying not to look like a dying guppy. He was past feeling hungry, wondering how much longer his strength would hold out.

*God, please make it end.*

He sunk into a whirlpool of despair, slowly losing the will to live, the will to fight for survival. His jaw went lax and the rebreather fell from his mouth, sinking into the depths. He gulped water, coughing to clear his throat. Rolling onto his back, he tried to float. He struggled, his arms feeling like rubber. Flailing like a headless chicken, his strength began to ebb and his arms refused to obey his commands.

He lost consciousness, fading into an abyss of dark dreams, lost hope and terror.

ᘐ∞

Barclay McKenner ambled about like he was touring a museum, poking his head into things and satisfying his innate curiosity. The gray alien followed him closely keeping a short distance away. Barclay couldn't help but glance over at him from time to time, feeling the same love he might have for a Labrador retriever or a pet cat. Oddly enough, he felt the same emotion back from the strange alien being, as if he were the pet instead of the master.

They came to a space ship swarming with activity. Gray beings were doing some kind of repairs. "What's this all about, Bub?" he asked his gray companion.

The gray said nothing but Barclay suddenly knew the ship was being cannibalized for the material it held. There was a pile of scrap sitting nearby. He hefted a piece of it trying to decide if it was metal or plastic.

He suddenly knew it was both and neither, a hybrid material both solid and invisible. Well, not invisible, more like it was dimensionally stretched. To say it was like a window, solid yet clear, would not begin to describe it. He looked over at the gray and knew the answer. Just as you could heat metal and turn it to a liquid, this material could be raised to a higher state of matter, to a point where it transcended three dimensional matter.

He looked over at his gray friend and knew again. A pilot could direct his life force into the material causing it to increase its rate of vibration, and like some kind of sublimation, it would move to a higher form of matter without going through intermediate states. The beings inside the ship could do the same, passing between different realms as easily as humans went from room to room. With the ship and crew raised to a higher plane of existence, the ship was free to travel without the limitations of a linear universe. There were rivers of energy at these higher levels. A clever pilot could surf these streams and, with minimal effort, quickly take the ship anywhere in the universe. Once at a destination, the reverse could occur and the crew and material would again descend or even elevate to a suitable dimension where it would be solid and able to interact with beings on that level.

"Any more questions?" It was the humanoid again. Barclay wondered where he came from so suddenly.

"Too many," said Barclay. "Is this what it's like to be abducted?"

The humanoid smiled. "We do not abduct humans. They actually agreed to work with us. Often they are not conscious of that decision, but we nonetheless have an agreement."

"Why abduct, I mean, work with them?" asked McKenner.

"Like your scientists, we collect data. We are very interested in the effects of food preservatives, pollution, stress, and other things on the human body."

"So are we," said Barclay. "Why not share your research?"

"It's not good science to interfere," he said. "It requires we remain objective and make observations. The mere act of observing sometimes skews the results."

"True," said Barclay. "Is that why you keep your presence a secret?"

"Your governments know about us," he said. "Recently they have released documents and information that proves they have known about us for some time. We have tried to work with them in the past, always with little success."

"Why is that?"

"Fear," he said. "Humans resist anything new. Also, your literature and films are filled with stories of creatures from outer space invading the Earth and subjugating humans. How could you reach your full potential and forge a relationship with us given that myth?"

"Things are changing," said Barclay. "Many humans are enlightened and willing to accept your friendship."

"Yes," said the humanoid. "Given the failures of the past, we have begun to make contact with individuals and groups that accept our presence and our purpose. Also, we are not the only extraterrestrial species. There are actually three major groups, humanoids like myself, insect like races, and those that resemble animals. Some beings do not even have a body. They exist as pure energy."

"What can you do as energy?"

"Actually, a lot. High energy beings live just as fully as you do. Moving in and out of the Divine Source of all life, they learn and grow like any being. "

"What about these gray beings? Are they a form of galactic life as well?"

"Of course," said the humanoid. "They are actually bred to be our companions and servants. Their bodies are much denser than ours and more adapted to moving in places like the Earth where dense matter exists. We can even transfer our consciousness into them when necessary, allowing us to extend the time we spend in coarse, lower dimensions. Speaking of that, I will ascend soon. As I explained earlier, it is difficult for me to maintain a presence in this state."

"Well, then, thank you for your effort."

"These things we speak of have been explored by your people. The ones we have worked with write about their experiences. There are many journals and documents available for you to consume. We have been an integral part of your history and will continue to be."

Barclay nodded. "I see," he said. "You never told me your name."

"We do not have names. We just *ARE*," he said. "You can call me whatever you like. The name is a point of reference for you, not me. I have no ego to feed."

"I understand," said Barclay. "Thank you."

"You'll be leaving soon. Amanhatayotep will coming to get you. You should wait for him by the entrance pool. Buddy will show you the way."

Barclay turned toward the gray being who smiled back at him.

"Buddy!" The humanoid laughed. "You and your nicknames!" He spoke to Barclay's gray escort. "Well, Buddy, show him the way."

The humanoid disappeared, fading again like sunlight at the end of the day. There was a surge of love from the gray alien, warm and inviting. Barclay wanted that feeling to last. He was drawn into that aura, following Buddy as they made their way through the maze of ships and material.

# Chapter 18

## Food for Thought

Fear swept through Cameron Singh. *Oh, no. I forgot to close the opening*, he thought. *Anything and everything seeking shelter can wander in here.*

The jaguar growled again as it looked around the room. Singh sat perfectly still, calming himself as best he could. He took slow, quiet breaths, quelling his fears.

Without warning, the animal lunged, leaping toward him.

Singh ducked and the animal shot over his head. He heard a squeal and turned. Blood dripped from the jaguar's mouth as it clamped down on the remains of a rat. Pieces fell on the ground in front of it. Using its powerful paws, it toyed with the remains for a moment until it lowered its mouth and ate the rest. He could hear the bones cracking in its jaws. The giant cat spit something out on the ground, his claws toying with the ragged pieces of meat again.

Sing breathed a sigh of relief but it was not over yet. The animal squared off in front of him staring him down. It licked it's mouth, the tongue sucking the last bit of blood from around its jaws. It licked its paws and Singh got a good look at the massive claws that had trapped the rat so quickly. *Will I be next?*

He thought about what he would do, how he could defend himself. There was a knife in his backpack, but it was across the room behind the jaguar. He went through a number of things he had learned to do when confronted by a large cat. Don't run, try to make yourself look bigger by waving your arms, act dangerous, show no fear, hold your ground and fight.

"It is not my destiny to be eaten by a jaguar," he said out loud. It was more of an affirmation than a statement.

"Actually, I am an ocelot," said the animal.

Singh opened his mouth in amazement.

"It's okay," said the ocelot. "I'm not going to eat you. Humans taste terrible. Rat makes a fine meal."

"Are you seeking shelter from the storm outside?"

"No. I'm here to teach you."

Singh asked, "Are you my spirit guide?"

"You might say that, but I am more like a memory."

"What do you mean?"

"I am a part of your past, present and future."

"Are you real?"

"What makes you think I am not?"

Singh reached out to touch him. The giant cat jumped back.

"Don't do that," said the ocelot. "You'll force me to leave."

"You are a hallucination," said Singh. "I must have ingested some of those drugs in that urn I opened."

"You're right about one thing and wrong about the other." said the ocelot. "You definitely ingested some of those drugs."

"It's okay. They were meant for you." It was Ixpetz, standing nearby, laughing. He spoke to the ocelot. "How are you, Tlacoocelotl?"

"Doing fine," he replied. "Not as good as him."

"Poor Cameron Singh," said Ixpetz. "You haven't figured it out yet, have you."

"I was just about to," said Singh.

"Of course you were," said Tlacoocelotl.

"For someone who claims to have superior Atlantean powers, you sure are dense," said Ixpetz.

"It's his ego talking," said Tlacoocelotl. "I haven't had time to teach him about the rule of isolation."

"What rule is that?" asked Singh.

"Oh, so now you want to learn," said Tlacoocelotl. "Before, you just wanted to prove I was real."

"That doesn't matter anymore," said Singh. "You're real. You're real. Tell me about the rule."

"The rule of isolation," began Ixpetz. "While our spirits inhabit these physical bodies, we are isolated. Matter on this level is so dense, it makes it difficult to relate to one another. The focus is on ourselves, our bodies, our problems. We forget our common origin, we forget that we are spiritual beings having a physical experience, not the reverse."

"What makes you think I do not know this?" asked Singh.

"Because you are dense," said Tlacoocelotl.

"And your ego will not allow you to," said Ixpetz. "You think you know everything."

"I don't think that," said Singh.

"Of course you don't," said Tlacoocelotl. "You're a perfect being."

"I am," said Singh.

"And there is your flaw," said Ixpetz.

"Obvious to everyone but him," said Tlacoocelotl.

"Now, now. Don't fault him for that," said Ixpetz. "Our flaws are often like that. I can't see my own. Maybe you can see them. Would you care enough about me to tell me about them?"

"Who's judgment shall I use?" asked Tlacoocelotl. "Who is to say what is a flaw?"

Singh shook his head. "You're obstinate, mysterious, and irritating," he said to Ixpetz.

"And so, you have described yourself," said Ixpetz.

"I am not obstinate," said Singh. "Or irritating!"

"I am you and you are me and so you have described yourself," said Ixpetz. "Have you considered that these may be the characteristics of the perfect Cameron Singh?"

"He still doesn't get it," said Tlacoocelotl.

"Well, there you have it," said Ixpetz. "And who among us is without flaw?"

"The gods have clay feet," said Tlacoocelotl. "At least they do when they are in physical form."

"Is this what I'm here to learn?" asked Singh.

Tlacoocelotl and Ixpetz both laughed. "No," said Ixpetz. "You should have learned that a long time ago."

"What then?"asked Singh.

"Patience, patience, what's your hurry," said Ixpetz. "Besides, there's a storm outside. You can't go anywhere."

"Wait a minute,"said Cameron Singh. "If you are me, then I should know everything you know."

"I agree," said Ixpetz.

"Then, why don't I?" asked Singh. "My mind is fuzzy on this."

"That's because your soul sets up these exercises and dramas," said Ixpetz. "I told you we are spiritual beings having a physical experience. Or did you think you ran this show?"

"Well...

"See what I mean," said Tlacoocelotl. "Ego."

"You did your best," said Ixpetz." You're a good teacher, you just have a dense student."

"You keep saying that," said Singh. "You're so insulting."

"If I am you, as you pointed out, then perhaps you should accept this as self criticism."

Singh let out a snort. "You are my past," he said.

"Past, present, and future," said Ixpetz. "Did you forget that time is a linear invention that exists solely in this dimension?"

"Very dense," said Tlacoocelotl.

"I don't know how we got off track," said Ixpetz.

"His ego," said Tlacoocelotl. "He took over the whole conversation."

"Yes," said Ixpetz, turning his attention to Singh. "Stop trying to be clever and listen to me. In non linear time you and I have acted together. You are my brother and my soul fragment. In the eternal now we must act together again. Time only has meaning for the beings incarnate. My promise has become your promise."

"I don't understand," said Singh.

"Listen to my story, and perhaps you will remember," said Ixpetz. "Our village was far away but I traveled here several times with my father. He wanted to show me this ancient and sacred place. Even then it was an ancient place, hidden in the jungle just as it is today. It has still escaped detection for that reason, but I fear that will not be true for long. Your modern techniques are probing the Earth as never before. Her secrets are slowly being extracted, just like her life giving water, and her precious oils."

"I do what I can," said Singh. "Most of us do."

"Me and my kind, the beings you call animals, have no voice in your decisions," said Tlacoocelotl. "Do you speak for us and in our behalf? Do we not have as much right to this world as you do?"

"He's right," said Ixpetz. "You must do more. Be their voice in the very least."

"I will," said Singh. "I promise."

Ixpetz nodded. "Let me continue then. Our people had high spiritual principles. They considered themselves artists, believing that the lives we lead are our art, our expression. They knew we humans are always dreaming, even when we are awake, and so they dreamed big. They became experts in metals, pottery, agriculture, and masonry. They built this place, along with many structures in this part of the world. They were warrior spirits and they prospered and grew, conquering and spreading their influence. This is our heritage, Cameron Singh."

"I still don't see what this has to do with me," said Singh.

"Quiet! There were two types of priests at the time. Men like my father who followed these ancient teachings. They were thinkers, teachers, and healers. Then there were the men of ritual who had spiritual training, yet were taken in by the dream. The power they yielded over men's lives captivated them, and soon all they could do was serve that power. They were the manipulators, the powerful, the butchers. I was sad for them, to be trapped like that, for these were not the dreams of sacred men, but of hollow men. Under such guidance the people grew far from true spirituality.

"When the conquerors came to this land, I was a young man. Despite the brutality of our priests and our warriors, the Conquistadors prevailed. We were not prepared for the violence that they would go through to take our sacred gold, crystals, and cacao. As mighty as our people once were, we were destroyed, subjugated, and broken. It was the will of the gods, punishment for our arrogance."

"Ego?" asked Singh.

Ixpetz smiled. "Have you ever heard of the Toltecs?"

"Yes," said Singh. "I have always been interested in them." He felt his mind shift. "Of course. No wonder I could understand the writing on the walls. This is one of their temples."

"A very special one," said Ixpetz.

"The Toltecs disappeared almost overnight, didn't they?"

"They did not disappear, they ascended. The conquerors helped to release them from the dream of this world. They knew the day would come. That is why they prepared for it. That's why they built this temple in the beginning, as a way to the end. Things have now come full circle. Time for you to do your part."

"And what is that?" asked Singh. "What am I supposed to do?"

"I wish I could tell you," said Ixpetx. "Our soul set this drama up. I've done my part. I guided you here."

Singh looked over at Tlacoocelotl. The big cat answered, "I can't help you either. I'm here for Ixpetz, your other soul fragment."

Singh turned back to Ixpetz, but he was gone. He turned back the other way towards Tlacoocelotl and he was also gone.

Cameron Singh sat alone in the empty, dimly lit room, more perplexed than ever.

# Chapter 19

## The Rescue

The wind intensified, the surf pounding the beach mercilessly. Manny's beach bar was taking a hit. The wind had ripped a hole in the roof exposing the inner beams. Caroline watched the damage on the wall monitors. Several cameras had gone dark, victims of the storm's anger, as if photographing it would steal it's soul. She continued to watch, drawn in like a rubbernecker to an accident, she could not look away.

She thought she spied something. The camera was shaky, hard to make it out. "Look at monitor seven," she said. "Is that a body washed up on the beach?"

"It's moving," said Stine. "Whoever it is, they're alive."

"It may be the wind just blowing them around," said Darius.

"Either way, there's a human being out there," said Juliana. "We have to do something."

"He's not the only one out there," said Stine. "Look, someone's attempting a rescue. There's a tall man heading there."

"It's Kransky, the village peace officer," said Darius.

"He's crazy," said Caroline. "Doesn't he realize the wind will blow him away?"

"Too late to tell him that," said Darius. "Contact Dr. Rampa. Tell him to expect one, possibly two, casualties."

"It's okay," said Caroline. "He's got a rope tied around him."

"Kransky's a big man," said Darius. "I don't know if he's up to fighting this strong wind."

Outside in the storm, Kransky's feet sunk in the soft sand as he

117

fought his way to the victim. Rain had soaked the beach. The waves were choppy, the tide unusually high. The wind came mostly from his side, often clocking unexpectedly in the opposite direction. The victim lay in shallow water. Kransky waded through the water, his feet sinking deeper in the sand making his task even more difficult.

The peace officer bent over and hoisted the limp body onto his shoulders in a fireman's carry. He had tied a rope to the railing near the stairs that led to the beach. It helped guide him back towards the shelter. Slowly, pulling on the rope for support, he trudged through the sand, the added weight causing his feet to sink even deeper.

Once on the concrete steps, he struggled, fighting against the wind that threatened to push him back into the sea along with his burden. Each step seemed to take more and more effort.

At the top of the stairs he was met by Roberson, a fellow peace officer. Roberson had run a line leading from the railing at the top of the stairs to the blockhouse shelter where Dr. Rampa waited with his emergency medical team.

Kransky stumbled, then quickly caught his balance and staggered ahead. Roberson tried to support him. The ground was slippery and the wind ruthless. Together they worked their way along the rope line towards the entrance of the bunker.

Dr. Rampa and a nurse were waiting for him in the corridor with a gurney. Kransky dropped the victim on it wishing they had one for him too. The nurse steadied him, letting the tall man rest against her shoulder. He was wet and soggy from exposure. Roberson had moved ahead, grabbing towels for the two of them.

Kransky turned towards Dr. Rampa. "Is he going to be okay?" he asked.

The physician bent over the victim. "Good Lord," he said. "It's one of our own. Notify the Think Tank that Franklin Van Dorn has been found."

# Chapter 20

# Time Runs Out

"The wind has stopped," said Darius. "How long do you think we have?"

"I'm not sure," said Caroline. "The eye is oscillating. Maybe thirty minutes."

"We'd better get busy then," said Darius.

"Look at the monitors," said Stine. "People are leaving the shelters."

"Specialists headed for their tasks," said Manny. "Power experts, refrigeration specialists, HVAC technicians, the entire staff of the compressed gas plant. All part of our coordinated effort."

"Looks like some of them aren't specialists," said Caroline. "They're ambling and looking around like tourists."

"Pass the word, do not let the general population exit the shelters yet," said Darius. "It's not safe. This is only the eye."

The sirens sounded the warning signal again. Some people returned, clustering around the entrances to the shelters, as safe as their curiosity would allow.

Manny went up to Caroline. "This is my cue to go. I need to take my place in this operation. Wish me luck."

"Take this instead," said Caroline. She stood up, put her arms around him and kissed him, uninterrupted for once.

Manny was breathless. "Thanks," he said.

"I need luck, too," said Stine.

She laughed, broke her hold and gave him a sisterly peck on the cheek. "That's enough," she said. "The eye is here. It's our lucky moment. Let's make this happen."

Manny smiled, grabbed a backpack and walked away.

"I'm going to join the LRAD technical team," said Stine. "We'll start our operation at once."

He walked off as a small group of section chiefs joined Caroline, Juliana, and Darius at the table. They set down computers, hand held communicators, papers and documents as they took seats around the table.

"Okay, Darius," said Caroline. "The village is completely within the eye wall. It's now or never."

Darius gave the order. "Fire up the molecular springs. Bring the torus to full generating power."

Kennedy was one of the newcomers seated at the table. "Already done," he said.

"Are the teams in place?" he asked.

"HVAC team ready," said Brubaker.

"High pressure team prepared." said Douglas.

"Juliana, contact Gaia," said Darius. "Tell her we are ready."

They heard a low, bass sound echoing through the village. "Ah, Stine has deployed the LRAD. Any affect so far, Caroline?"

Caroline answered. "Minimal. Pressure is changing, fluctuating. The eye wall is still tight, still mostly over water. Complete landfall is imminent."

"HVAC teams are in place and operational. They report their mission is fifty percent complete," said Brubaker. "Refrigeration specialists say they're ready to power up."

"What about the gas plant?" said Darius.

"My team is in place and standing by," said Douglas.

"Power is approaching maximum." said Kennedy.

"Divert power to the refrigeration teams," said Darius.

"Power diverted," said Kennedy. "We're stabilizing the grid for phase two."

"Whenever your team is ready, Brubaker."

He gave the command. The team had set powerful coils in place, connecting them to the steel pier, effectively turning it into a cold plate. As the power surged, the steel began to cool. Ice quickly formed, the tide high and close to the deck of the pier. Similar teams had arranged to cool other things in the village, including metal structures like the open domes, certain buildings, and even large pieces of art.

They watched impatiently. Caroline continued to monitor the statistics, mouthing them from time to time. "Temperature dropping slightly," she said. "Barometric pressure increasing. Still no noticeable impact."

Stine reported in. "We're focusing the LRAD over the ocean, hoping to punch a hole in the seaward side of the storm."

"No effect so far," said Caroline.

"Have we heard from Manny yet?" asked Darius.

"He's ready to deploy," said Cara.

From a hidden hanger in the mountain came a fleet of anti gravity hover cars, flat ones used for moving freight. Each was equipped with its own power generator. They spread out, taking up positions near the base of the hurricane wall. Wind threatened to pull them into the storm and the drivers struggled to keep the cars stable. Beams of anti gravity particles flowed as operators focused them on the base of the storm.

Brubaker went blank, muttering a simple "What the?"

"This was my idea," said Darius. "They're trying to lift the storm off the ground."

"It's not going to work," said Brubaker.

Caroline glared at him.

Brubaker glared back. Suddenly on the monitor, they watched a large rock become unhinged, beginning to float on the air. "Look," he said. "See what I mean?"

The rock shuddered, a huge piece of stone that was hundreds of feet high and just as wide. Without warning, it moved, as if swatted like a tennis ball in mid air.

The hover cars were on it, the teams operating the generators aiming it at the rock. Under their direction, it was flung out into the sea where it landed a short distance offshore.

Brubaker picked up his communicator and switched the channel before speaking into it. "I see what you're doing, Manny, but it's not going to work."

"What do you mean?" came the answer.

"Gravity has to do with mass," said Brubaker. "Just look at what happened. You're shooting gravitons at water droplets. What makes you think they have the mass to absorb gravinometric energy?"

"We weren't sure," said Manny. "It's an experiment. We had to give it a try."

"Stick to particle physics," said Brubaker. "I'm the resident expert in gravity. You should have consulted me."

"It's okay, genius," said Manny. "We have a backup plan."

Brubaker was smug. "Basic law of physics, chum," he said. "You of all people should know that."

"I'm a scientist," said Manny. "That's what I do. Perform experiments. It was a good idea, worth trying."

"Like I said. Stick to physics. Any second year student could have figured out that water won't absorb anything bigger than an electron."

Manny was about to deliver a clever retort when a better idea struck him numb. "Yes!" he said. "You're right Brubaker. You're so right.

Water will absorb an electron. Thanks for the idea. Over and out."
He switched channels, contacting his teams. "Nice try," he told them.
"This was a good test, but gravity is not the answer. I briefed you on
plan B. Now is the time to implement it. Put on your thermal
pressure suits."

Chatter followed, some full of excitement, some full of relief.

"Glad to move on. I didn't feel safe that close to the wall of a storm,"
said one operator.

"I kept getting sucked in and spun around," said a driver.

"You were too close," said another. "The further away I moved the
more stable I became."

"Duh, but when we did, the graviton stream decreased exponentially
with distance."

Manny finally interrupted. "That's enough. Switch your generators
from gravity to force field. I'll join you if I can, but I've got one more
thing I want to try."

"Okay Boss," came the reply. "See you up top."

Manny watched the nearest hover cars rise, then focused his eyes
downward. He piloted his own hover car down, parking in a safe
garage near a low, flat building. As he walked towards it, he became
mindful of the eye of the hurricane. It was deceptively quiet, the
wind gusting occasionally as it swirled in the dead space. He heard
birds chirping in the nearby trees. He wondered if they followed the
storm or sought shelter in a hollow tree or a cleft of some rock. He
sighed, noticing how his shoulders drooped and how each step came
with effort. It was an oppressive environment, heavy with humidity
yet deceptively calm. He sensed the slight feeling of low pressure
sapping his will to continue. It was like fighting a psychotic
depression. He began to lose faith in his ideas.

He stepped over fallen branches and debris blocking his progress.
The building was directly ahead. "I'm committed," he said out loud,
more of a self affirmation than a declaration of intent. "It's too late
for me to join the airborne teams." He opened the door to the

building, turning a massive power switch that hummed as it slowly lit the hallways.

"Manny we're almost in place," came a voice on his communicator.

"I won't be joining you," he said. "I'm busy. You're in charge, Frank. Coordinate your effort with our storm expert in the Think Tank, Caroline Garmin."

There was a wisecrack before silence. "Okay by me. I don't mind working with your girlfriend."

Manny blushed.

Darius stood beside Caroline in the Think Tank staring at the wall of monitors. There were signs of debris everywhere: fallen trees, leaves and rubbish pushed up against fences, overturned and loose lawn furniture. A long piece of fabric awning was caught up in palm tree.

"We can see everything but what we need to see," said Darius., thinking of the air cars and the teams aboard them dressed in pressure suits. "Tracking has them at 30,000 feet."

"I would have liked the view," said Caroline. "Manny's vehicle was the one with the cameras. Now he's off doing something else and all we get to see an empty parking garage."

"I'll see if I can get a hold of him," said Darius. "I also want to know what he's up to."

Caroline continued to watch the monitors, listening to the chatter between the hover cars as they hit the 40,000 foot elevation mark. She imagined what it would look like at the top of the storm, a tight eye defined by dense clouds. The updraft of air would disperse in the high altitude wind, spreading rain clouds in the distinctive circular pattern. The teams in the anti gravity hover cars were taking a big risk. One tilt in the wrong direction and they could be whisked away or be toppled and fall out of control.

Darius returned. "He's going to use quantum entangled electrons."

"What?" said Caroline, her voice making it sound like a puppy yelp. "What is that even?"

"I'm not sure," said Darius. "It has something to do with particles being linked no matter how far apart they are."

"I can understand that, but how does it relate to a hurricane?"

"I'm not sure," said Darius. "We're willing to try anything at this point. Besides, we learn as much from our failures as we do our successes."

"How does he even know about this stuff?"

Darius looked surprised. "Didn't you know? Manny has a masters degree in Particle Physics from the University of Helsinki and a doctorate in Quantum Engineering from the Julius Maximilians University in Würzburg. He used to teach at MIT."

"He never told me that," she said.

"He's modest," said Darius.

"I just hope he knows what he's doing," said Caroline.

"So do I," said Daius. "But when it comes to quantum mechanics and particle physics, Manny is my choice. Whatever he has in mind, it should be interesting."

# Chapter 21

## City in the Mists

Cameron Singh sat alone in the temple contemplating his experience. Was it the drugs? Was he really visited by his former self and a mysterious ocelot? He had awakened that morning, sure he had something to find, something to retrieve. He studied the object in the center of the alter. "Is this it?" he asked aloud.

The sound was absorbed by the walls. No echo. He moved his lantern closer to the wall, studying the pictures and the writing. "Maybe this will help."

It didn't.

Frustrated, he did what he always did when he had a difficult puzzle to solve. He meditated. He sat down facing the alter, facing what seemed to be the only object of interest in this room. He focused on the dark round thing sitting in the bowl, a piece of it visible above the rim, looking like a small dome. Was it a jewel? Rock? It certainly was heavy and stuck in place. What purpose did it serve?

These and other questions surfaced as he contemplated them. Deep in a trance, Cameron Singh began to drift in thought. He closed his eyes, seeing the object in his mind's eye.

Time passed, innumerable, measured only by the soul. When he opened his eyes, the object was glowing, the room bright with White Light. The writing on the walls was visible, two depths to it. When he studied it he could see two meanings as well. It was as if, in English, how an F can become an E, P a B, a C an O, and so on.

The purpose of the temple was now clear. Images showed priests using the light of the object to heal people.

"You have succeeded," said Ixpetz. Singh looked for him but it was only his voice. He smiled, feeling a sense of accomplishment.

"Almost," said Ixpetz.

"What?" asked Singh. "What else is there to discover?"

"According to our soul, that's your job," said Ixpetz. "You should know already."

"Most of us are born into this world not knowing our purpose," he said. "It takes years of schooling and decades of growth just to get to the point of understanding. I would appreciate a little help."

"Must I tell you everything?" said Ixpetz. "What of life's mysteries? Do you not like surprises?"

Singh turned back to carefully studying the writing on the walls. "This is not Nahuatl."

"Very good," said Ixpetz. "So it is not Aztec. Keep reading."

"It can't be Mayan," said Singh.

"Why not?" asked Ixpetz.

"Could it be Toltec?"

He heard a soft purr beside him. Turning, he saw the ocelot. Singh jumped, The big cat yawned, displaying his usual, bored disinterest.

Singh stood up, reading the walls in more detail. His meditative state had not ended. As if sleepwalking, he wandered over to the alter. Pressing his hands to the sides of the bowl, he felt impressions that easily fit his fingers. He closed his eyes, his hands gripping the bowl that contained the heavy jewel.

He could feel the presence of something. Fighting the urge to open his eyes and look, he continued gripping the bowl. A warm feeling swirled in his gut. More than an emotion, he could feel that something was building in his abdomen. Like an old style space heater, waves of energy began to flow from him, moving out towards the alter.

"He's doing it!" said Tlacoocelotl.

Singh was startled. He opened his eyes. The room was filled with light. Directly ahead of him, the mysterious jewel floated above the bowl, the source of the light. He smiled, turning to look at Tlacoocelotl. Light flowed through the room, visible and in currents. They circled around Tlacoocelotl. The image of the large jungle cat blurred. His legs elongated and he stood up. In another blur, he became human looking, his face shrinking as it took on the characteristics of Ixpetz.

The former cat, now Ixpetz, looked at him and smiled. "Yes, you're doing it," he said. The light continued to glow and circle him. He changed shape again, this time becoming a woman.

Cameron thought he recognized her, she seemed very familiar. She laughed, then blurred to become another person, a man wearing a loincloth. Another blur and he became a priest adorned in the robes of a Cardinal or even a Pope.

Singh watched in amazement, transformation after transformation. In the final change, what was once Tlacoocelotl became a golden being. The light in the room seemed to be drawn into him, absorbed from every corner. There was a sucking sound as the last of the light faded from the room, drawn into the golden being standing before him.

"Hello, Cameron Singh," said the Golden Being.

The light in the room came from the Being now, a glow that cast no shadows. Cameron looked over at the bowl. The jewel floated in the air above it.

"Who are you?" asked Singh.

His question was met with laughter. "You do not recognize your own Oversoul?"

"My what?"

"Congratulations," said the Golden Being. "You have been successful."

Singh looked over at the floating baseball. "I thought that was my goal."

"You are welcome to try to take it with you," said Goldie. "I have the feeling that it will not want to leave."

"I tried to lift it," said Singh. "It was heavy."

The Being laughed again. "As I said."

"What did I come here for if not that?" asked Singh.

"Gifts are not always something physical," said the Being. "Can your hands hold my vision? Is knowledge not something that can also be recovered?"

"I guess so," said Singh. In that moment he realized why he was here. "You!" he said.

The Golden Being urged him on. "Yes..."

"My soul." The words found a new meaning.

"You do not know everything, Cameron Singh," said the Soul.

"You are my past, present, and future," said Singh.

"Not just that," said the Soul. With that, there was a sudden rush of air and the being turned into light. The light filled the room for a moment before it circled around Singh where it was sucked into his body. Singh glowed for a moment and then the lights went out. The light from his lantern seemed dim and faded, all that remained. The stone was back in the bowl. He reached into it, trying to pry it free, but it would not move. "What?" he said aloud. "Don't you want to come with me?"

He heard a voice in his head say, "I am as much a part of this temple as you are a part of your soul."

"What then?" asked Singh.

"Take this experience with you," said the voice. "It is as tangible and real as anything in this room."

"Yes," said Cameron. "I understand."

"The storm outside is abating," said the voice. "It is safe to go."

Cameron gathered up his things and put them in the backpack. Using his lantern, he followed the passage out again, careful to avoid the traps. Outside, a gentle rain fell on him. He felt like it was washing away the sins of the world.

Back in the meadow, the aircar was intact, as if a tree had never fallen on it. He heard the voice one more time as it said, "Remember us. Remember our teachings. Dream big. After all, humans are always dreaming, even when they are awake. Accept that much as truth, Cameron Singh."

# Chapter 22

## End of the Line

The LRAD continued to pummel the wall. It seemed to have no effect as the wind whisked away any hole it may have created. Technicians observed a splattering of water against the wall, almost like a child slapping a puddle.

"LRAD is losing its effectiveness," said an operator. "It wasn't designed to function for this long. We need to shut it down to recharge the capacitors."

"Do it," said Stine. "How much dead time do we need?"

"At least thirty seconds, maybe a minute before firing it again," said the technician.

"Okay," said Stine. "For the next series I want the beam redirected. Aim at a spot over the steel pier. Maybe the cold plate will help it out."

"Aye, sir."

"Winds are gusting at one hundred and seventy," reported Caroline.

"That's down from before," said Darius. "Our efforts are having an impact."

"Don't be too sure," said Caroline, "Storms always lose speed when they make landfall. Look at the storm surge on the monitors. Unusually high tides. Manny's place is surrounded by water."

They stared at the monitor images. Sure enough, water was everywhere. Tourist hotel swimming pools were underwater. Street signs poked through flowing rivers. You could barely see the rooftops of the small shops that lined the beach and sold snacks and rented gear. The lagoon was overflowing its banks, debris floating on the dark surface. Trees and jungle plants were surrounded by water, making the village appear to be in a swamp.

Darius shook his head. "You're right. We're still not in the clear."

"At least you built above the flood plain," said Caroline.

"Everything but the beach front resort," said Darius. "The first floor is equipped with floodwalls. All the electronics and infrastructure are on the second floor and the rooftop enclosures."

Hope filled his heart as he looked at another monitor and saw a church group assembled outside a shelter. On another monitor a circle of people chanted. Near the beach, a small assembly of locals were praying as they cast flower petals and other offerings on the turbid waters.

Caroline's voice interrupted his thoughts. "Manny's crew is in place," she said. "They're at fifty thousand feet."

"Top of the storm," said Darius. "Give the order. Tell them to commence operations."

The anti gravity cars circled about, their power generators focused on building a force field. Pilots kept the craft steady while the operators carefully knit the forming energy fields into a single unit.

"It's growing," reported Frank, the team leader.

Looking out over the storm, it was a visionary form of heaven, thick bands of clouds reaching out in all directions. Below them was a monstrous hole that stretched all the way down to the ground. Above, bright sunlight illuminated it, making it seem surreal, almost like an artist's canvas.

"You should be here," he said into his communicator.

"I wish I was there," said Carolyn. "Take a picture for me."

"None of us brought a camera," he said. "Manny had the recording equipment in his air car. What's he up to anyway?"

"We're not sure," said Caroline. "Something to do with particle physics."

She heard Frank laugh. "Sounds like Manny," he said. "He spends most of his spare time in the physics lab at the Village University."

"Am I the last to know this?" she asked.

"I'm surprised," said Frank. "He's always bending my ear at the bar trying to explain his theories to me."

"I guess we had better things to discuss than particle physics," said Caroline.

Polite conversation was interrupted. "We're experiencing some turbulence here," said Frank. "The force field is unstable."

"I imagine it's like trying to press the lid down on an open, boiling pressure cooker," said Darius.

"A bit stronger than that," said Caroline. "More like trying to cap an active volcano."

"Yes," said Darius. "One made of air, with a wall of wind instead of stone."

"A moving wall of wind," said Caroline. "Sucking up moisture like a giant soda straw and throwing it out at fifty thousand feet."

"We're lucky nobody has capsized," said Darius. "Hold on! I'm getting a message from Manny. He says to check camera U57." He went to a wall monitor and made some adjustments using a thin line of controls along the bottom of the frame. It flickered and he saw Manny rolling a cart on the outside walkway of the physics lab. He parked it and locked the wheels. He spoke into his communicator headset. "I'm almost ready, Darius. I just have to load the collinator with my radioactive sample."

"A colli-what?" asked Caroline.

"Collinator," said Manny. "A lead storage container with a hole in one end."

Caroline stood beside Darius watching as he worked. "What is that?" she asked.

"I'm not sure," said Darius. "Something he made out of two broken

Geiger counters and an old, pre-digital xray machine."

Caroline turned and looked at him. Darius just shook his head.

The LRAD sounded again, the low bass sound pushing against the wall of the hurricane. Above the steel pier a misty rain splattered rhythmically. In the operations center the technical team had adjusted the beam to pound against it like a battering ram. The technician modified the cadence. "Take that," he said.

"What are you doing?" asked Stine.

"Giving it a headache I hope," he said.

Meanwhile, Frank was in a panic. Caroline put him on the two way loudspeaker for Darius to hear. "We're losing stability," he said. "We were able to deploy a pretty good spread of force field, but we can't top it off. Every time we push the field towards the wall, the winds shred it, tearing it apart like a wet napkin."

"Hang on," said Caroline. "Manny looks like he's getting ready to try something."

They couldn't tell what he was doing. Fiddling around with some equipment on the cart, there was nothing to see. "What's happening, Manny?" asked Darius. "What are you doing?"

"Creating a stream of quantum entangled electrons," he said.

"Whatever that is," said Caroline.

Nothing appeared to be happening. Manny stood next to the cart adjusting things. "What's he doing?" asked Darius.

Brubaker was beside him. "He's creating a beam of quantum entangled electrons. What did you expect? They're small and invisible to the naked eye."

The beam of electrons shot outward and into the storm. Water molecules absorbed the electrons and with them an ionic charge. "Just about there," said Manny. "Now to measure them." His hand reached down to the cart and flipped a switch. There was no sound, no hum of scientific apparatus, nothing to reveal that anything was

134

happening.

"I don't know what he's doing, but the windspeed is dropping," said Caroline.

"Could be the effect of capping the storm, too," said Darius. "Don't discount the effect of the crew deploying the force field."

Caroline's communicator let out a chirp. "It's not us," said Frank. "Something else is going on up here."

Above the clouds at fifty thousand feet the view was even more fantastic. Below lay the storm, the eye churning in an angry circle of power. The hover cars struggled to keep their positions, pushed occasionally in a hapless and roundabout manner. Above them, a stream of lights had appeared.

"UFOs," said Frank.

Darius turned to Caroline. "What?" he said.

"Unidentified Flying Objects," said Frank. They're breaking formation. I wish you could see this."

"So do I," said Caroline.

"They appear to be helping us," said Frank. "Our force field is expanding."

Caroline checked her readings. "The pressure is rising in the eye," she said. "Over nine hundred millibars now." She paused a minute before reporting, "Nine twenty five... Nine thirty. Something is working, Darius."

The LRAD continued to pound in the distance. On the monitor, Manny stood by his cart. On the steel pier, the HVAC team focused diligently on their task. Above the storm, nobody could tell what was happening as Frank continued to talk about the appearance of UFOs.

"It's our friends," said Darius. "We have agreements with the extraterrestrials, but I didn't think it extended to this."

"Don't forget Gaia," said Juliana. "She is doing doing her part, along with the prayer groups."

"Pressure still rising," said Caroline. "Windspeed has dropped again. We're at a category three now."

Darius smiled, the first smile of the day. Caroline continued to report, but the tension had faded. Pressure continued to drop. Outside, what was once the eye expanded, clouds dissipating in all directions. The waves began to grow calm. The water that had filled the lagoon and flooded the beach flowed back into the sea, leaving ripples in the sand as it left. Pools remained full to capacity, but the water around them disappeared. Walkways slowly emerged from retreating waves, lines of leafy debris and sand left behind.

Caroline heard laughter through her comm link. Frank and his team were celebrating as the pressure continued to rise. Before long, the skies cleared, turning to thick clouds that were quickly moving away. The rain bands evaporated as the sun emerged from behind them. Outside the shelters cheers went up, praises to Gaia and the bold residents of the community that had risen to their defense.

"Category one now, Darius," said Caroline. "Atmospheric pressure returning to normal."

"I wish you could see it up here," said Frank. "The aliens are leaving. Seems they believe they are no longer needed."

"How can we thank them?" asked Caroline.

"Help needs no thanks," said Darius. "They heard our prayers and our plea. Help always arrives when you ask for it."

"But... aliens?" asked Caroline.

"Help doesn't always come in the form we imagine, but it comes," said Darius. "All you have to do is ask."

# Chapter 23

## The Verdict

Though it was quiet and powered down, Randall remained in the locked chamber. The tribunal of judges had returned and he felt their power over his life. He remained calm despite his predicament. He was about to hear his fate. It would not be so bad having to live among these people. They seemed to need him as much as the village.

Astra took her seat in the middle again, Reena and Wezley beside her. "We have considered everything, Randall of the surface world. Are you ready to hear us?"

"Yes, please." He pushed against the glass expecting to be released from his coffin. They watched him struggle for a moment. Wezley shook his head in disgust but Astra and Reena were both smiling back at him. "No point in trying," he muttered to himself. "You got me."

"You are not a prisoner here," said Astra.

"Could have fooled me," said Randall. "Then why am I restrained like one?"

"If I told you it was for your benefit, would you believe me?" said Astra.

Randall pushed against the glass. "Probably not."

"We have decided you must live by your own words. You talk about reunification, about joining our two civilizations together. We do not know if this is possible. If it is to happen, it remains in the hands of men like you. We know you are probably better suited for your world than this one. Here you would find only leisure and contemplation, worship of the highest order. We are not saying that you cannot find these things in your world, only that it is more difficult.

"If reunification lies in our future, then it is up to you, not us. We can plan for such a day, but you must also be ready for it. Meanwhile we will bide our time, watch and observe, and hope that you become the noble beings you were meant to be. And so, to this purpose, we release you from any obligation here. The spirit of the law has been met, although not the letter of the law."

"So that's it?" asked Randall. "I'm free to go?"

"We will send you on your way now," said Astra.

"Thank you for the medical treatment," said Randall. He tried to leave the box, but found it sealed. "You said I'm free," said Randall. "Are you going to open this prison?"

"That is no prison," said Wezley. "It is a device we use. Through our meditations, we have gained some control over time and matter. We will show how much in a minute. Meanwhile, know we are watching your world, hopeful, like you, but ever watching. Good luck."

The tribunal closed their eyes. They began to glow, their auras bright and visible. Their crown chakras opened like lotus flowers gathering energy as easily as a funnel gathers rain. Power surged in their hearts, a glow emerging as a bright light reached towards the box and surrounded it. There was a flash and then Randall lost consciousness.

# Chapter 24

# The Debriefing

Despite the catharsis, the operations center was still a buzz of activity. The Think Tank met one last time to close the door on this event. Cara took notes as the discussion began.

"Okay," said Darius. "Time to put our heads together for the debriefing and create the after action report."

"What's that?" asked Caroline.

Stine smiled. "We always have this meeting. It's our way of putting closure on the event. We talk about what we did, document it, and try to come up with ideas on how we might do it differently the next time."

"Will there ever be another event like this?" asked Caroline.

Juliana spoke now. "We can only hope not," she said. "Imagine what would have happened if the hurricane was created over the Village, appearing without warning."

"It would be hard for that to happen," said Caroline. "Hurricanes need a lot of warm water to feed their growth. They usually form far out to sea."

"We didn't get much warning," said Stine. "The appearance of this one was sudden and unpredictable."

Darius interrupted, pulling everyone back on topic. "Okay, so this may happen again, even though it is a slight chance. It's all the more reason to put our heads together and analyze this one."

"That was too close," said Manny. "Despite our strong building practices, it could have been the end of the Eighth Day Village of the Sun."

"I doubt it," said Darius. "The population was in the shelters. People make a village, not buildings."

"I still don't understand what happened," said Manny.

"Neither do I," said Caroline. "We'll be studying it for years."

"How can we tell what worked?" said Manny. "We did so many different things all at once."

"Maybe that's what we need to do again in this situation," said Darius. "As humans, we are always more successful when we work together."

"I can't say if my work had any effect," said Manny. "I wouldn't know how to begin to tell if it did."

"I'm sure it did," said Caroline. "What were you doing anyway?"

"Yes," said Darius. "I want to know too."

Manny looked into empty space for a moment, trying to gather the words. "Basically, I created two streams of electrons that are related, or entangled, as the name suggests." His hands were moving, his words needing help translating what was in his mind. "The electrons are quantum related and are not independent of each other, despite the distance between them. I shot a beam of these particles into the storm where they were absorbed. Once they were absorbed, I measured them. The act of measuring quantum entangled particles causes an irreversible wave function collapse which changes the original quantum state. The effect is instantaneous. My theory was, as the particles collapsed and returned to their original state, they would dissipate whatever absorbed them. In this case, I was hoping the water molecules would absorb them, become ionized, and collapse the storm when I measured them."

There were a few blank stares around the table. Darius looked over at Cara. "Did you get that?"

"I have the words down," she said. "Whether I understand it or not is another thing."

"You measured them?" asked Caroline. "And that made them do...

whatever you said?"

"It's one of the paradoxes of quantum mechanics."

"Okay, then," said Darius. They continued on, discussing and debating the various strategies they tried. Cara took it all down. Later she would create and file the final after action report.

"Well, this was a true group effort," said Darius. "But we were never in any real danger. As long as we remained sheltered we still would have survived."

"What worked then?" asked Manny.

"We'll probably never know," said Caroline. "And it's in the past now. By a miracle we survived."

"More than a miracle," said Juliana. "Gaia was with us. She helped blow it out as well."

"That might explain something," said Caroline. "I noticed the strange change in the upper atmospheric winds. It's almost like the jet stream was diverted. I don't think it's ever been this far south."

"Never underestimate the impact of planetary consciousness," said Juliana. "We can either work with Gaia or against her. You see what's possible when we work with her. Why anyone would choose to work against her is beyond me."

"Juliana, you and Darius mentioned something about weather control," said Caroline. "Do you really think it's possible?"

"Of course it's possible," she said. "Didn't I tell you that President Whiteweather confirmed it?"

Anger erupted over Darius, a volcano of hate. "I daresay we just saw an example of it," he said, his words coming out through clenched teeth. "He's the cause of all of this."

Juliana squinted her eyes as she stared at him. "And we managed to thwart him again."

"He'll keep trying," said Darius. "I hope we're ready for the next attempt. We are up against a powerful enemy."

Stine interrupted, breaking the tension. "Well, as you say Darius, this was truly a group effort. Our thanks to everybody who did their part."

Juliana stared at Darius and he softened. "I've thought a lot about it," he said. "I have a saying. There are too many coincidences to be a coincidence. That holds true in this case. Accepting that, I conclude he is the one man with the motive and the resources to do this. Juliana agrees with me on this, don't you." He stared back at her, powerless for the moment against his anger.

"I see where this is going, Darius," said Juliana. "We all know what you know, that T. Harmon Rothschild is likely behind this. Look at what your anger is doing to you. Instead of malice, I suggest we all take a moment of prayer for Harmon Rothschild." She looked around the table, gathering her support as she pushed back the emotion of anger in favor of compassion. "To live in the darkness like that, the shadow of the soul, so far from human nature, so far from love. It is a thing to be pitied. Malice would only bring you to his level, and you are a better man than that, Darius."

"Anger is a forest fire, burning away your good intentions," said Manny.

"Here, here," said Stine. "For all his wealth, I would not trade places with Rothschild. He's going to be even more frustrated when he finds out we survived this."

"And saved countless people who would have suffered as the hurricane moved inland," said Caroline.

"Insult to injury," said Juliana. She chuckled. "Can you imagine the temper tantrum."

There was general laughter until Darius said, "There's no telling what he will try next. We must be vigilant."

"There is no better strategy," said Juliana. "We must let Rothschild know we support humanity. We are judged as a species en masse. We support the idea that every individual deserves a voice in this world, and more importantly, that their voice deserves to be heard."

"Very idealistic, Juliana," said Caroline.

"I am guided by my ideals," said Juliana. "Navigators of old relied on the stars to guide them. Like the stars, I can never touch my ideals. They are there to guide me."

"Freedom demands vigilance," said Stine.

"We can ask Singh to keep an eye on Rothschild for us," said Juliana.

"Has he reported in?" asked Manny. "I'm worried about him."

"I'm worried about a lot of people," said Darius. "Singh, Randall, Barclay, Franklin. What's the status on Van Dorn?"

"The Doctor reported a while ago," said Stine. "He's exhausted, malnourished, dehydrated, and suffering with Post Traumatic Stress Disorder, but under Doctor Rampa's care he'll be okay."

"There's no better doctor in the Village," said Darius.

Tamara from Human Services arrived. "Shelters are reporting in," she said. "They want to know if it's okay to leave."

"The hurricane's gone," said Caroline. "It's a beautiful day outside. Don't see why there's any reason to stay indoors."

"Sound all clear," said Darius. "Have the damage assessment teams start their survey. "

The sirens blared again, this time a welcome sound. People began to leave the shelters, nervously emerging to look at the damage. Debris was everywhere, mixed with fallen tree limbs, garbage, leaves, trash cans, and anything that wasn't bolted down. Piles of sand were pushed up against some of the buildings. Without being told, citizens began cleaning the sidewalks, shoveling sand, and pushing wooded debris into big piles where teams were collecting them.

Cameras were repaired and replaced. The few buildings that had lost power were restored to their former status. Lawn chairs that had been tossed around like loose paper were collected and returned to the beach where groups of workers were raking the soft sand and returning it to pristine white.

Offshore, a large rock stood vertical, poking out of the ocean like a cracker stuck in a bowl of dip. It rested quietly on the sandy bottom of the sea where it settled even deeper as the gravitons slowly dispersed. Waves beat against it, white spume spraying in the air, giving it a noble appearance, a reminder that once again the Village had prevailed against all odds.

The birds were everywhere, their chirping filling the air with hope. Gradually other animals were spotted. House cats, dogs, lizards, and mice emerged from hiding to explore their surroundings. Leah the white leopard, a common site in the Village, returned to her perch near the public sex fountain.

In the operations center, people were securing their workstations and cleaning up before they left. Darius pulled Caroline aside before letting her leave.

"I owe you an apology," he said.

"Huh?"

"I misjudged you," he said. "As you can see, I'm quick to anger at times. I don't handle the tension and responsibility as well as Baba Randall. He would normally be in charge. I don't know what we would have done without your extensive knowledge of weather. Your contribution to the Village will not be forgotten."

"Yes," she said, a little hesitant. "It will all be written into the after action report, right?"

"Let me rephrase that," said Darius. "I won't forget your contribution to the village and to the Think Tank."

In the short silence that followed, Caroline said, "Perhaps I misjudged you, too."

Darius offered her a smile, a welcome sight to anyone. He extended his hand. "Friends?" he asked.

She pushed the hand aside and gave him a hug. Darius smiled. Forgiveness can wash away anger like a cool shower. He broke the embrace and smiled, the last of his anger finally gone. In his heart, he tried to be indifferent about Rothschild, knowing that the opposite of hate is not love, but indifference.

"Now, if you'll excuse me," he said. "I think there's someone else who wants to give you a hug."

Manny stood nearby waiting his turn. As Darius broke his embrace he spoke to them. "You're a member of the Think Tank, now," he said. "Both of you." He turned to Caroline. "I know you don't live here, but there are other ways you can serve. As for you," he said to Manny. "There's no going back. Cara can handle the Information and Planning section from now on. Your seat over here becomes permanent."

Manny smiled. He had been avoiding it. Why, he didn't know. He had been asked to join numerous times, even by Randall himself. Now, the decision was made for him. He thought of an old saying, something his father had said. He could hear his voice now in his heart and in his head. "We all have a destiny. It is our job to embrace it and fulfill that destiny."

# Chapter 25

## All Clear

Randall awoke in the cave. It was raining outside, though not hard. A trickle of water flowed where a river of mud once gushed. He was wedged in the rock. He reached up and felt a lump on his head. Rubbing his thigh he sensed the same dull ache that he had experienced at the hospital inside the hollow earth. He was able to move his leg, glad that he didn't have a broken femur.

He crawled up to the cave entrance and looked out. The storm seemed to have dissipated. The sea was calm again, the tide slowly emptying the pools and raceways that once held deadly currents and angry waves. All that remained were some clouds above, even now turning from gray to bright white.

He climbed out of the cave and made his way down to ground level. He sunk to his ankles in the wet sand, his feet settling in two pools of muddy water. "Can't stand still in these conditions," he muttered to himself. "I better get moving." He started to walk along the beach, heading north towards the Eighth Day Village of the Sun. He took his wet sandals off, it was more comfortable walking with bare feet in the sand. The air was warm and humid and his damp clothes stuck to his skin like wet cellophane.

He rubbed the knot on his head, trying to remember how he got it. There were other things he vaguely remembered, fading slowly like bits of a dream in the morning dew. The memories of his experience were being stored deep in somatic memory, someplace where it would be difficult for him to recall. The hollow earth again became a myth to him, something he had read in books and considered, but deemed less important than other things in his life. "Did I dream it?" he asked himself out loud.

With those words, the last of the code was written away, erased like a whiteboard, like a mistake that had never happened.

There was a nudge at his side and a whinny. "Anji," he said, glad to see his giraffe had found him again. He pet her gently, walking beside her, talking and asking her what she did to weather the storm. Finally he climbed back onto his mount. She shuddered, turning her long neck to look in all directions. Randall found the reigns in his pocket. He put them on Anji, gently patting her on the neck before shouting, "Hyaa!"

She took off running. With the sea on one side and the mountains on the other, Randall was once again in paradise.

# Chapter 26

## Shattered Dreams

Rothschild seethed. "What's happening?"

Simian stared at the monitor. The hurricane had barely hit shore when it began to dissipate. They watched the circular bands of clouds scatter into fast moving lines of cover, dark spots indicating rain was turning to light mists. "I don't know, sir," he said.

"Gort, check the news feeds," said Rothschild. "I want a report."

Gort disappeared.

Simian stared at the money. He reached over to grab it.

"Oh, no," said Rothschild. The fat man got up from his comfortable chair and pulled the plate away. "The demonstration is not over," he said.

"I did my part," said Simian. "A category five hurricane struck the exact coordinates you specified. That was our agreement, was it not?"

Rothschild sat back down. "It was," he said reluctantly. "You'll be paid. Be patient. Before I relinquish the money, I need to know what happened."

"I can't explain it," said Simian. "The hurricane was at full force. How could it possibly disperse so quickly?"

"I've seen their technology," said Rothschild. "I watched them destroy a tsunami with one of their infernal devices."

"Them?" asked Simian. "There were people at this site?"

"A small village," said Rothschild. "A nuisance if you ask me."

"I didn't realize that," said Simian. "I thought it was just some empty coastline."

"It's well hidden, built beneath trees and in between mountains. Bigger than it appears on the satellite imagery we've been looking at."

Simian stared at the money, his brain calculating the cost of human life again. "How many people?"

"It doesn't matter," said Rothschild. "Do you think it was a failure of the weather control?"

"That's a possibility," said Simian. "These coordinates are slightly out of range of our satellites. The Government's tests were focused on a remote area of the Pacific. They weren't designed to cover a wide area yet."

"Why over the Pacific?" asked Rothschild. "If you could make it rain in the desert, why not focus the equipment over our own land. There must be comparable areas of low population, even near Tonopah where you work."

"I don't know, sir," said Simian. "It wasn't my decision."

"Unless the Government wanted to weaponize it from the beginning," said Rothschild, following his own twisted reasoning. "Once over the Pacific, it's much easier to move the satellites to China, or Indonesia, or the Middle East, or any enemy. Why not all of them? Death, like the sun, would rise in the east."

Simian felt a shadow cross his soul, a shiver that left him empty and cold.

Rothschild caught himself. He changed the subject, burying the thoughts in the deep folds of his brain for later consideration. "So, you think the satellites were out of range?"

"I'm not sure," said Simian. "Tinker knew the network better than me. He knew how it all fit together. His software touched every part of the system. He could have easily figured it out."

"Well, I guess we won't know anytime soon, then," said Rothschild. "Tragedy about that boy getting mauled by a bear. Not my fault. I agreed to keep the wildlife intact when I purchased this place."

Gort entered the room followed by a man named Gustav. "I've been monitoring the storm, just as you asked," said Gustav. "It's gone. Mexico has been spared."

"How?" asked Rothschild. "Where did it go?"

"It never moved inland," said Gustav. "The news is full of it. A miracle, they say. Churches are overflowing in Mexico City. People are praying and giving thanks."

"The churches were full before the storm, crammed with refugees and superstitious people," snorted Rothschild. "Religion. The pablum of the masses."

"Perhaps God actually spared them," said Simian. "I hadn't considered that."

"That may be one possible explanation," said Gustav.

Rothschild was angry. "Not the one I'm looking for."

"You mentioned something about stopping a tsunami," said Simian. "Is it possible the people of that village found some way of neutralizing the storm?".

"A category five hurricane?" asked Gustav. "How is that possible?"

"If somebody found out that our nation was developing weather control as a weapon, they might have started to build the opposing technology," said Rothschild. "There are spies everywhere."

"But a category five hurricane?" said Simian. "I assumed, like a bowling ball, once we took aim and sent the storm on its way, it would have no choice but to hit its destination."

"And that it did," said Gustav.

Simian found himself staring at the money again. Gustav had agreed with him, he had done what he promised. The test was a success. But why did the storm die? Tinker could have told him why. Tinker knew. A true humanitarian, he knew a lot more than just engineering.

"The storm may have dissipated when it hit land," said Gustav. "But residents of the Eighth Day Village of the Sun surely felt the impact of the category five winds as it approached."

"I've thought of that," said Rothschild. "At least that's something."

"And don't forget the storm surge," said Gustav. "Ten to fifteen feet high tides were predicted."

"Yes, yes," said Rothschild.

"You have something against these people?" asked Simian.

"That's my business," said Rothschild. "Here." He pushed the plate back across the table. "Take it," he said. "It's only money."

Simian lit up with greed. He fingered the bills, flipping through them and stuffing his pockets full. He started to imagine all he would do with his newfound riches. He saw his reflection in the bottom of the empty plate. He heard Tinker's voice in his head. "Are you happy now?"

Rothschild growled, more menacing than any bear. "Get out of here, all of you. I have some thinking to do."

They stared at the boss before turning to leave the room. Simian reached for the computer. "Leave that!" demanded Rothschild. "Go!"

Simian turned, following the staff through the thick double doors.

The fat man sat back in his chair after they left, his face twisted, full of anger and dismay. He downed the last of the drink in front of him, throwing the empty glass across the room. It shattered against a wall, broken shards scattering across the polished floor.

Gort heard the sound from outside, wondering if he should call the housekeeper. He thought better of it. Why risk the wrath of Rothschild? He slowly walked away, escorting Simian to his room before heading towards the servants quarters and the relative safety of his private quarters.

# Chapter 27

## Broken Pieces

The worst damage by far was Manny's beach bar. The tide had been merciless, waves battering the walls, wind ripping at the roof. The forces of nature had broken through, scattering the contents of the building and tossing things around like a child playing pick up sticks.

Manny stared at the twisted pile of wood and bamboo. The metal roof that once adorned the top of the bar was gone, a piece of it fifty yards away crumbled against the wall of one of the tourist hotels. The bar was intact, covered in debris and dirt. Sand blocked access to everything. A steady stream of things, glasses, cups, bottles, and plates, lay in a line where the tide had tried to pull them back into the sea.

Carolyn saw the tears in his eyes. She said nothing, letting him experience the loss to the fullest. Grief comes in stages. He would let her know when it was time to move on.

Something came unhinged inside. He turned away from her, the tears overflowing like a broken toilet. His jaw was slack, his eyes empty. She slowly moved close and put her arms around him. They held the embrace in silence for the longest time. He finally pushed her away, wiping the wetness from his eyes.

"Despair is a terrible emotion," she finally said. "I only know one cure for it."

"What would that be?" he asked.

"Despair wants you to be quiet and still, motionless as you kill every joy you ever had. You just want to lie down and die."

Manny felt the heaviness, the weight of everything on his shoulders. "True," he said. His body went slack, the will to move becoming difficult.

"That's not going to happen," she said. She squeezed him hard, snapping him into attention, pulling him into a position of good posture. She pushed his round shoulders back and said, "The only cure I know is to take a walk," she said. "Despair wants to keep you down. The only way to fight it is to get up and move."

He heard the truth in her words.

"How about we go for a walk?" she asked. "I'd like to see what else is damaged along the coastline."

She held his hand, pulling him along like a difficult child. He finally gave in, walking down to the tideline where the gentle sound of the waves crashed against his inner walls.

She was right. After walking a short distance, he began to feel better. She could tell, and she squeezed his hand and gave him a knowing smile. He began to walk faster, the will to lie down and die fading as quickly as the storm had faded.

Ahead they heard a noise. As they rounded a bend they saw Randall in the distance, his shouts urging Anji onward. He slowed as he approached them. Manny couldn't help it. He smiled, glad to see his friends. Anji stopped, lowering her head for Manny to pet her.

Pure love can cure anything, whether it comes from a strong partner or a trusted animal. He let go of Caroline's hand and reached up towards the giraffe.

"Good to see you, Manny," said Randall. "Although it looks like Anji is happier than me to see you."

Manny rubbed her neck. "I'm glad to see her too." Anji sputtered, a spray of spittle falling on Manny's shoulder.

"All is right in the world here," said Randall. "How did the Village make out during the storm?"

"The usual," said Manny. "We sheltered in place until it moved on."

"He's lying," said Caroline.

"No I'm not," said Manny.

"Okay," she said. "He's not telling you everything."

Manny looked at her. "I didn't want to get caught up in details," he said. He turned to Randall. "We used a combination of refrigeration, force fields, prayer and meditation to stop the storm."

"Don't forget particle physics," she added.

"Really?" said Randall, his face frozen in astonishment. "I missed a lot."

"What about you and Anji?" asked Manny.

"We hid out in a cave. At least I did. Anji found her own shelter and we were reunited after the storm. Is all well with the Village?"

Caroline nodded no as Manny spoke. "Some things need to be rebuilt but overall we survived another calamity."

"You'll have to give me details," said Randall. "Right now I want to get back and get something to eat."

Anji sputtered.

"I'm not the only hungry one," he said. "Hyaaa!" and they were off.

As the hoofbeats faded Manny turned to Caroline. "I can't thank you enough," he said.

"About what?"

"You were right about walking. I feel so much better."

She hugged him and pulled him closer. "There's a few more things I might suggest," she said.

He was about to say something when she planted a big, wet kiss on his lips. "Enough talk," she said. "Let me show you another cure." She gently pulled him off the beach and towards the jungle where she took off her wrap and laid it down on the sand. They sat down together, Manny forgetting all about storms and particle physics.

"Is this what you had in mind on that deserted island where you were going to take me?"

∂∞

Time stood still. They emerged later, thirsty and hungry. The walk back to the Village was peaceful. He was unusually quiet with nothing to say. She indulged him, realizing that despite his outside appearance, the grief was still strong within him. She stared into the thick jungle, leaving him to his thoughts.

The animals had returned. They heard birds and monkeys chattering, occasionally the roar of something larger. As they approached the Village there were shouts, sounds of hammers and power tools. As they moved closer he couldn't believe his eyes.

People were everywhere. The broken remains of Manny's beachside bar had been cleared and piled neatly. Two women were removing nails from wood and stacking it aside. There were tables set up. Others were gathering things from the beach and bringing them there to be washed, dried, and neatly stored in totes. The bar had been uncovered, the broken beams above it put back in place. Three men were positioning new metal roof panels and banging them in place. Randall was up there too, hammer in hand as he flashed a wide grin towards Manny.

"What's going on here?" he asked.

Officer Kransky stepped forward. "I guess the community decided what needed to be rebuilt first."

"Of all the silly priorities..."

"That's what I said," said Kransky. "Damage assessment teams suggested many more. The Village tram needs repairs and the yoga dome took a hit, but somehow this seemed more important."

"Why bother?" asked Manny, still slightly bitter with depression.

Darius was behind him. "For one reason," he said. "It's your work, your dharma. This community needs you Manny, more than you will ever know."

"The bar served it's purpose," he said.

"Does that mean you're going to focus one hundred percent on the Think Tank?" asked Darius.

"I don't think that's what he meant," said Caroline. She turned towards him. "I heard you kept this job to mingle with the tourists, looking for the next Mrs. Manny DuBois."

Manny laughed, a bitter sound filled with despair. She pulled him closer. "Maybe it's time to stop looking," she said.

The sound of hammering interrupted his thoughts. Despite his inner, broken drama the place was being put back to normal. He realized he was surrounded by a sea of love, a community that cared for him and for everything he did. He felt another hand on his shoulder.

"You helped me when I was going through a bad breakup," said one person.

"I don't know where I could find a better smoothie," said another.

"You were here for me after my home caught fire," said still another. "I'm grateful to return the favor."

"Look, Manny," said someone. "Everything's not broken. This plastic cup is okay." He held it up for him to see.

Manny laughed at that, slowly letting go of his pain. He had no choice. The sea of love was all around him, keeping him buoyant and afloat. He looked into Caroline's eyes and tried to smile. He bent down, picking up a half broken decoration that had once graced his walls. He walked over to one of the remaining walls and gently hung it up. He went behind the bar and inspected the damage. Someone had swept the floor and wiped everything down. He opened the cabinets and looked at the array of bottles and flavorings. The freezer still had some ice in it. Turning back towards the crowd he smiled and said, "Does anyone need a drink?"

There were tears in his eyes again, she could see the wetness.

Despair had finally given way to joy.

He felt yet another hand on his shoulder, comforting and reassuring. He turned to see Caroline. "It will be okay," she said. He began to fill a glass with ice and she let go of him. This was just the therapy he needed.

"This is the price of survival," said Darius, a hammer in his hand.

The crew behind Darius was working hard. Juliana raised her arms in benediction. "If we rebuild anything it should be this," she said. "Your bar has always been a symbol to the community, a place where anyone could come for a bit of refreshment and some good conversation."

Lights came on. "We got power!" somebody shouted. Manny spotted two members of the refrigeration team carrying a large tote of ice. They set it down behind the bar. The sound of churning blenders filled the air and soon smoothies and iced drinks were circulating faster than you could say Category Five.

The area around the bar was quickly cleared, stools set upright and tables arranged with chairs and centerpieces. It looked like Manny's was open for business.

He found bins of chopped fruit, clean glasses, and plenty of ice. He did what he always did, asking customers what they wanted, creating treats and eats for the crowd.

Carolyn sat on a stool watching him. Rebuilding was a slow process. There were still two open walls to the bar and a huge pile of sand where the lanai once stood. Children were playing on the dunes nearby, another sign the crisis was over. She looked out over the ocean, catching a glimpse of dolphin leaping. Lights came on in the nearby tourist hotel and the sound of music filtered down to them.

Philippe arrived, stepping behind the bar to work beside Manny, filling requests and making his job easier.

Caroline laughed. "You were supposed to be here earlier today," she said.

"Sorry I'm late," said Philippe. "What can I get you?"

Before she could answer, Manny nudged him aside. He placed a tall drink in front of her, topping it off with a straw, a piece of fruit, and a decorative umbrella. She looked up into his eyes. Around him the noise continued, but it didn't matter. He picked up his own glass from behind the bar. Raising the glass to her, he offered a toast.

"To us."

Now she was the one crying. "I'll drink to that!"

# Chapter 28

## Home at Last

The sun was setting in the west casting a golden glow across the azure sea. Neptune swam into the shallow waters near the inlet at the Eighth Day Village of the Sun. The dolphin felt the fresh water mingle with the salt before turning to swim away.

Barclay let go of his dorsal fin and popped the rebreather out of his mouth. "Thanks for the ride," he said.

Neptune leaped in the air, splashing water and chirping like a happy dolphin. Then he dove under the sea and disappeared.

"Until next time," said Barclay. He turned on his back, kicking gently, watching the sunset as he began a leisurely paddle towards the shore.

He heard music, drums and shouting. He turned, feeling sand just beneath his feet as he bobbed in the waves. The sun had set and dusk took over in its place. There were tiki torches and a huge fire on the beach, another burst of gaiety as the crowd joined in celebration again. Barclay smiled. What better place to come ashore than Manny's.

There was a drum circle on the beach around the fire, beating an island beat. Outside the bar there was a long table with a half picked buffet spread. He took a plate from a pile and filled it with roasted vegetables, papaya, and mango salad. A piece of sweetbread topped the heap of food. As he turned he saw Caroline Garmin approaching.

"Barclay?" she asked. "Barclay McKenner? Is that you?"

"In the flesh," he said, stuffing a piece of sliced pineapple between his lips.

"You've been missing for three days," she said.

"Three days," he said. "Wow. It seems like less than that."

"What are you doing here?" she asked.

"I could ask the same of you," he said. "Three days ago was supposed to be your last day in the village. I'm just as surprised to see you as you are to see me."

She laughed. "I'm still leaving, just winding down after the excitement. Besides, I wouldn't miss this luau for the world."

"A luau?" he asked. "Did they roast a vegetable pig like they usually do?"

"Didn't you see the spit over the fire?" she asked.

"I saw the buffet table first. I'm famished." he stuffed a forkful of salad in his mouth and munched.

"I'm amazed how they get so much vegetable matter to look like a wild boar," said Caroline. "Really throws off the tourists and carnivores."

"Chef Aaron and his vegi-meat," said Barclay. "The man's a foodie maestro."

There was another cheer and the sounds of revelry from inside the bar momentarily drowned out the drum circle. Barclay turned and started to walk away.

"Where are you going?" she asked.

"Home," he said. "Where I can eat in peace."

"You need to go inside first," she said. "You've been missing. People are worried about you."

"You'll tell them I'm okay," he said.

"It would be better if it came from you," she said.

"I'm not up to it," he said.

She took a deep breath. "I came here to fix a plate for Manny. Keep me company a bit longer." She took a plate and began putting an assortment of food on it. "You have to come to the bar and tell us about your adventures. Franklin Van Dorn just finished a few minutes ago."

"Franklin? What do you mean? He's alive?"

"Yes," she said. "He washed ashore during the storm, a little exhausted, but alive and kicking. Come inside. People are getting up on the karaoke stage and telling stories about the storm and how they survived it. It's very therapeutic. And now we have reason to celebrate! You've the last one on the missing persons list. All present and accounted for."

He smiled. "Karaoke stage? When did Manny put that in?"

"The original Manny's was destroyed by the storm. It's been rebuilt, bigger and better. You have to come check it out." It was obvious she would not take no for an answer.

She took him to the bar and sat him down in her empty seat. "We're all anxious to hear your tale."

He continued to gobble down food with the manners of a street dog in winter.

"Eat, first," she said. "I wouldn't want you talking with all that food in your mouth."

"Barclay McKenner," shouted Manny from behind the bar. He set a drink down in front of the hungry man.

Heads turned. "Barclay McKenner?" someone shouted.

"Barclay," yelled Van Dorn, parting the crowd like Moses as he made his way across the room.

It was as if winter had set in. Barclay McKenner sat there frozen in silence.

McKenner put his fork and plate down. He hugged him, tears in his eyes. "I thought you were gone."

Franklin pat him on the back. "You too. What happened out there?"

"You wouldn't believe it," said Barclay. "First, let me fill you in on what I learned about our friend Neptune. By the way, that's not even his name."

He never finished his story. People clapped, shouting with revelry, urging McKenner to take to the stage and share his ordeal with everyone.

"Give the man a minute," said Van Dorn. "He's been through a lot."

"Haven't we all," said Barclay. "Haven't we all!"

## The End

Thank you for reading! I hope you enjoyed this book. Please let me know by writing a review on line. It would motivate me to do another Eighth Day Village of the Sun Saga. I write what people want to read, and the only way to know is through feedback. Here are a few more books that you might enjoy.

The first novel in the *Aliens vs. Dinosaurs* series. Sixty five million years ago giant beasts fought each other for dominance of the herd. One monarch has a vision of a better world in which dinosaurs cooperate and live in peace. But that peace is shattered when hostile aliens from another planet challenge the dinosaurs for dominion of the Earth. They collect the small ones, the children, taking them away to a distant laboratory where they can experiment on them and find new ways to destroy the dinosaurs once and for all.

King Rex finds his daughter is among the missing. As his world crumbles around him, as his enemies circle around him looking for weakness, he struggles to find a way to harness the power of flying without wings. His goal: to send an envoy of peace to the aliens and negotiate the release of the children. Failing that, to take the children back using an army of dinosaurs that have united behind him with one thought in mind: Rescue the children.

*Becky Jane: Memoir of an Incredible Life*

Written by Nick Delmedico senior, this book was a 2017 Human Relations Indie Book Award Gold Winner. In 2014 his wife was diagnosed with end stage esophageal cancer. He saw her through chemotherapy and radiation treatments, but it was not enough. Three years later when the cancer returned, metastasized in her lower gut, she refused treatment. He and his son left their jobs to take her on a final bucket tour.

This is their story, a family driving towards an inevitable destination that cannot be avoided. But if you live bravely, there can be many pleasant stops along the way.

### Sword of Fire

A little angel in heaven asks her father: "Do angels die?" He knows the truth, having survived the great war that separated Heaven from Hell. His brother Lucifer expected him to take sides against their Father, putting him in a moral dilemma. He instead joined the neutral angels, undertaking a mission to carry the Holy Grail out of heaven to a place of sanctuary in a sacred mountain. Thus begins a momentous quest through heaven and hell and all that lies between. He will cross-rugged terrain unknown to man; pits of fire, caves of darkness, and fallen angels out to destroy him and his band at every turn. Throughout this ordeal, one question keeps surfacing, a terrifying thought that he fears to face. "Do angels die?"

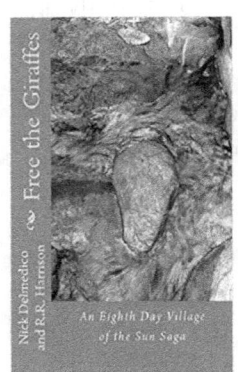

### Free the Giraffes

In the future we will have intentional communities, villages and cities based on humanistic ideals. They exist today, places where people choose different values to live by. The Eighth Day Village of the Sun is one such community projected into the future. Set beside the sea, the village has embraced spiritual and humanistic values. They are led by Baba Randall, a holy man who hears of the collapse of nations beyond the walls. Civilization is breaking down. Riots, shortages, war, and coups abound. A contingent of leaders is headed his way asking for help. Not all want help, some are ready to steal technology to maintain their control over the world's population. Will spirituality win out over the banal?

by Nick Delmedico

*The Nth Carlos*

A killer is loose leaving a trail of bodies behind that stretches across the country. The killer is bold, leaving many clues to his identity, but the evidence is conflicting. Police Detective Canfield has been assigned to the case. Canfield suspects that more than one person may be responsible for the murders. The FBI has their eyes on this case, ready to intervene and take over the investigation. The trail leads to an old man who tells him a unbelievable story of what happened.

Rich with drama, this story questions our motives and purpose in life. A short read, you won't want to miss the mind bending conclusion.

www.ingramcontent.com/pod-product-compliance
Lightning Source LLC
Chambersburg PA
CBHW051521170626
46811CB00002B/927